The key to saving the world could destroy him.

SHADOWED RECKONING

OLIVIA HUNTINGTON

World Castle Publishing, LLC
Pensacola, Florida
Copyright © 2023 Olivia Huntington
Paperback ISBN: 9798891260504
eBook ISBN: 9798891260511
First Edition World Castle Publishing, LLC, September 25, 2023
http://www.worldcastlepublishing.com
Cover: Cover Designs by Karen
https://www.cover-designs-by-karen.com
Editor: Karen Fuller

CHAPTER 1

John woke with a start, his cries piercing the pre-dawn silence. The echoes of screams still rang in his ears — the ghosts of his failure, relentless in their torment. Fumbling in darkness, his trembling hands found the bottle of whiskey on the nightstand. He brought it to his lips with desperation, not even wincing as the amber liquid seared his throat.

Sleep had granted no reprieve, only visions of the night that had shattered him. They came in fragments, visceral as memories day-fresh. The Dark Mark was leering down like some hellish moon. The heat of flames against his skin. The screams and sobbing, people running blindly to escape the carnage. But there was no escaping, not for John. He was rooted in place, utterly helpless as lives were extinguished around him.

He could still smell the smoke, choking and thick. Still feel the surge of dark magic crackling in the air. The details haunted him — a child's small shoe lying broken in the street, streaks of blood smeared across the bricks. And the bodies. Broken bodies strewn like discarded dolls. Blank eyes stared up at him in perpetual accusation.

You failed us, those empty eyes seemed to say. We died because you failed.

The visions tortured his soul. John pressed the heels of his palms against his sockets until starbursts exploded. But nothing could block out the memories. They were seared into his mind, raw and bleeding as though the destruction unfurled again and again on some endless loop of torment.

The digital clock read 3:17 a.m., but sleep would elude him now. John rose on unsteady feet, staggering through the dark apartment more by muscle memory than sight. He did not bother turning on a light — what was there to illuminate? Peeling wallpaper and threadbare furniture cast in shades of gloom. This dreary place was as hollow and ruined as his soul.

He stumbled into the bathroom, gripped the basin's counter, and glanced up at the mirror. The face staring back from the bathroom mirror was haunted, all sunken eyes and gaunt hollows. Days-old scruff patched his sagging cheeks, flecked with silver that had not been there before. His ashen complexion resembled a corpse pulled from the dark water. Deep lines of grief and horror were etched beneath his eyes.

With a guttural cry, John slammed his fist into the glass. Fissures spiderwebbed across his reflection but left the surface strangely intact. Drops of crimson slid down his knuckles, pooling in the sink below. The physical pain centered him, driving back the smothering darkness with brilliant clarity. Slowly, he breathed, focusing on the staccato drip into the basin until the red haze lifted from his mind. He splashed some water on his face before roughly bandaging his hand.

The bleeding had stopped, but the gashes still oozed as he shuffled to the kitchen. He tore open a new bottle of Jameson, indifferent to the hour. The whiskey had become as vital as oxygen or blood, the sole barrier between John and utter dissolution. He downed one burning gulp, then another before dropping heavily into a chair.

There on the table sat the damned letter he had been ignoring for days. His name and address were written in a neat feminine hand that conjured Claire's lilting voice. Another plea for help, no doubt. As if he had anything left to give anyone. As if he was anything but a hollow ruin. John let out a bitter laugh. Let the mages keep chasing their fool's hope. He would drink until he faded away entirely.

The streets were still hushed and empty as John stepped outside, the moon a waning crescent low on the horizon. He walked in solitude, collar turned up and shoulders hunched. Just another shadow drifting through the urban abyss. The anonymity suited him. He kept his eyes trained down, carefully avoiding the newsstand on the corner. But the headlines seemed to glare at him from the periphery of his vision.

Massacre In Diagon Alley. Mages Fail To Stop Rampage. Deadly Attack Exposes Flaws In Ministry Protections.

Ten years on, but still, the reports dredged up the gruesome details — homes collapsed to rubble, bloody maws where windows once housed cozy kitchens. Stores turned to char and ash. They tallied the numbers like ghastly statistics — eighty-seven injured, forty-six dead. Yet behind each number was a face, a life extinguished because he had been careless. Because he had failed when people needed him most.

John quickened his pace until the

newsstand was far behind him. But there was no outrunning this particular demon. Not when its fangs were sunk so deep into his soul.

The smell of stale beer washed over John as he stepped inside O'Leary's pub. Only a few die-hard regulars occupied the grim space. Old men with nowhere to go, nursing pints in the relentless pursuit of oblivion. They glanced up with darting eyes as John sat at the bar but looked away just as quickly when they recognized his face. He had become another fixture here at the end of the world — the disgraced mage who drowned his dishonor in whiskey.

"You're here early." The bartender's gravelly voice roused John from his stupor. He was a brawny man with a brawler's squashed nose and gnarled knuckles. John gave a noncommittal grunt, not wanting conversation. But the keepsake game banners and framed photos of laughing patrons marked the bartender as the gregarious type.

"Another all-nighter?" he asked, eyeing the dark hollows below John's bloodshot eyes.

John's mouth twitched with something too bitter to be called a smile. "Sleep and I aren't on speaking terms these days."

The bartender nodded sympathetically as he poured two fingers of Jameson into a glass. "Aye, I know a few gents like that around here. Plenty of demons to keep a man restless at night."

John tossed back the whiskey in one burning swallow. His hand trembled when he lifted the empty glass, silently requesting a refill.

"Thank you," John muttered hoarsely. He did not elaborate on the nature of his demons. There was no need. In this place so far from daylight, every man's torment wore plain across his face.

When the lunchtime rush filtered in,

their raucous voices grated against John's frayed nerves. He glanced around the pub through narrowed eyes. Laughter and easy smiles felt foreign to him now, artifacts of a life abandoned long ago. What right did these people have to their mirth when so many had perished choking on screams? When ghosts stalked John's every waking moment?

Their normalcy seemed obscene somehow. An offense against the immense toll evil had extracted from the world. From him most of all.

By mid-afternoon, the Jameson had worked its magic, swaddling John's psyche in gauzy cotton. The voices around him faded to a distant murmur. His limbs grew pleasantly heavy, their weight tethering him blissfully to the barstool. Nothing could touch him here in this cocoon of detachment.

But as afternoon gave way to evening, the liquor's grip began to loosen. Jagged reality crept back in as John slid off his perch and stumbled onto the sidewalk outside. He cocked his head back to welcome the light rain speckling his face. Anything to wash away the lingering haze of inebriation, leaving only pure sensory clarity behind.

He didn't make it far down the block before his roiling stomach seized control. John lurched into a nearby alley just as the Jameson forced its way back up his throat in a vile deluge. Bracing his hands against damp brick, he retched until nothing remained inside him but foul strings of bile.

When the heaving finally ceased, John collapsed against the alley wall, spent. He sat in refuse like a vagrant too broken for even a gutter. The soles of his shoes soaked up a week's worth of rainwater and piss, but he was numb to the discomfort and stench.

Because in his darkest moments, the ones he tried desperately to blot out with whiskey, the truth confronted him plain. He had no right to comfort or dignity, not after what his arrogance had cost.

John closed his eyes, surrendering to the bone-deep exhaustion weighing down his limbs. His chin slumped to his chest as clammy skin kissed cold brick. But rest provided no reprieve from the past that stalked his every moment.

Even with eyes shut tightly, he saw them — himself and his mage partner Miles grinning and smoking behind the holding cells, drunk on their early success. Two rookie hotshots brimming with swagger. The photograph was from the front page of the Prophet, right above the fold. He had kept a framed copy on his desk for years like a badge of honor. Until that desk had been cleared out by some Ministry lackey when the offices and positions they'd earned were stripped away.

"You're damn lucky they didn't toss you in Azkaban, traitor." Miles' words after the inquiry still rang in his ears. There had been genuine loathing there beneath the pain of betrayal. Perhaps a part of Miles wished they had locked John up and thrown away the key. It would have been easier than seeing his disgraced partner wander free each day, a living reminder of how profoundly they had failed.

When John staggered up from the alley sometime later, the streetlamps were aglow against the dusk. He shuffled down the sidewalk with his collar turned up, less a man than a ragged coat animated by sheer reflex. The city bustled around him — workers heading home, shop owners locking doors and pulling metal gates. Night's rituals proceeded as they should for all but those trapped in the past's grip.

Out here, amongst ordinary lives unfettered by regret, John was keenly aware of his apartness. He was an open wound oozing invisible toxins, destined to corrupt whatever he touched. He had proven that beyond any doubt.

As he waited at a crosswalk, the sorrows John worked so hard to muzzle crept from their cages. A young couple with a little boy in tow passed in front of him. The boy beamed up at his parents, swinging their entwined hands in careless delight. Love illuminated their faces as they smiled down at him. Something about the unguarded joy carved out John's chest.

That could have been you. It should have been. If only you hadn't ruined everything.

The memory ambushed him viciously — Marissa's beautiful face contorted in a scream as their apartment burned around them. The heat seared his skin as he clutched her limp body. Her belly was round with their unborn child. The boy who would never see first steps or birthdays. More bones for him to bury when the mages pulled them from the rubble.

The bile rose up in John's throat once more. He staggered into the crosswalk just as the light changed. Brakes screeched, horns blared, but the oncoming traffic barely registered. At least if a careening truck plowed him down, the pain of shattered bones might eclipse that pulsing from his heart.

But the cars swerved around him, leaving John untouched on the opposite sidewalk. Once, there were those who relied on him for their safety, who trusted he would shield them from harm. They did not know the man entrusted to guard them was a hollow sentinel, powerless against the dark forces lapping at their world. Not until it was too late.

As he shuffled on down the block, the familiar visage of the run-down Oakridge Apartments emerged — an architectural blight blockish and utilitarian as a warehouse. It suited him perfectly. Most of its residents had given up on better prospects long ago. They hid here among fellow outcasts, nursing their regrets and disappointments.

Inside his apartment, John sank onto

the couch without bothering to kick off his soaked shoes or turn on a light. He sat in the dark, drops of rainwater sliding from his coat to stain the already threadbare fabric. When grief pressed its claws into his throat, he almost surrendered to its seductive pull.

John sat staring into the empty fireplace, turning the possibilities over in his mind. The unopened letter from Claire lay on the coffee table, his name neatly printed on its surface. Another plea for help, no doubt. He scoffed bitterly. As if the mages had any use for him now beyond being a cautionary tale.

With a resigned sigh, John picked up the envelope and tossed it aside unopened. Its promises were surely hollow. Even if redemption lay at the end of this path, it was not meant for one so irreparably damaged. The man Claire hoped to save had died alongside his victims years ago, leaving only this wretched shadow behind.

John dragged himself to bed but found

no refuge in sleep. Visions of the night that ended everything still plagued him. Flames consuming Diagon Alley, its familiar facades reduced to rubble. The leering Dark Mark was again suspended overhead like some hellish moon. The doomed screams of the innocent rang out as they ran blindly from the carnage. But there had been no escaping their fate. Not with John frozen helpless nearby, all courage fled.

He awoke shivering and drenched in sweat as the first pale light of morning bled through grimy windows. John rose slowly, scrubbing a hand down his haggard face. He shuffled to the dingy bathroom and stared into the mirror at the ghost gazing back. Bloodshot eyes in bruised hollows. Sagging cheeks covered in graying scruff. Faded tattoos marking foolish youth. This feeble, ruined creature hardly resembled the mage who had tackled darkness unafraid. There would be no saving John now.

Resignation settled like stones in his

gut as he went through the motions of his morning ritual — dressing, making bitter coffee, avoiding his own hollow eyes in the mirror. He wanted to crawl back into bed rather than face another empty day. But reflex propelled him upright, kept his feet shuffling toward the future that held only further desolation.

In the living room once more, John's gaze fell upon the old photograph on the bookshelf. Faded and dog-eared, but his wife's smile still shone up at him, hopefully. Beside her, John's forever-young double grinned down at the blanket-swaddled newborn nestled in his arms. His daughter Lily was barely a week old when the picture was taken. That man had brimmed with fierce joy and promise. Would he even recognize the wreckage his choices had yielded?

John traced his wife and child's faces, overcome with echos of that bright, ephemeral happiness. He had been so convinced it would last forever. Fate had mocked him cruelly for such arrogance. Now Marissa was gone, and she had taken Lily with her before she could even speak her first words. His wife, his daughter, his... unborn son. All because he thought himself strong enough to conquer the darkness. He had failed.

Tears burned trails down John's gaunt cheeks. Even here alone, he despised this naked display of sorrow. But grief pierced his armor in these quiet moments when there was no drink or distraction or redemption to be won. Only the raw ache of irrevocable loss.

CHAPTER 2

John woke with a start, disoriented from another night of fitful sleep. He squinted against the gray morning light filtering through the decrepit blinds. For a long moment, he lay still, trying to shake off the haunting visions that plagued his dreams. John rubbed a weary hand over his face, feeling the rough stubble on his jaw. His mouth tasted like ashes.

With a groan, John hauled himself upright, joints creaking in protest. He sat on the edge of the sagging mattress, head cradled in his hands. The ghostly faces flickered through his mind again — men, women, children, all innocents. Their deaths weighed heavy on his soul. He should have saved them. He was a coward.

These daily confrontations with his past failures were nothing new. The horrors never left him, not completely. During the day, he could push them down and lose himself in mindless distractions to keep functioning. But at night, his defenses crumbled.

Sighing heavily, John forced himself to his feet. He shuffled to the bathroom, pointedly avoiding his reflection in the cracked mirror. He didn't need the visual confirmation of what a wreck he'd become. The man who had stared back at him once — honorable, courageous, full of conviction — was long gone. All that remained was a shattered shell going through the motions.

John went through his morning ritual mechanically — shave, shower, brush teeth. The motions were rote, almost robotic. As he toweled off, the jagged scar on his shoulder caught his eye, a permanent reminder of battles fought and lost. He quickly averted his gaze.

After dressing in rumpled jeans and a faded T-shirt, John made coffee. He welcomed the scalding bitterness. Anything to burn away the relentless memories for a few precious moments. With its flickering fluorescent lights, the spartan kitchen felt more like a prison than a home. He couldn't even remember the last time he'd had a visitor here. Few had reason to seek him out anymore.

A harsh knock at the door jolted John from his gloomy thoughts. He froze, mug halfway to his lips. No one ever came here, at least no one with good intentions. The knocking repeated, more insistent. John set the mug down with a clatter and grabbed his wand from the counter. He crept to the door silently, muscles coiled to attack.

"John?" Called a vaguely familiar female voice. "It's me, Claire. I need to speak with you urgently."

John froze. Claire? It couldn't be. He hadn't seen or spoken to her in nearly five years. Not since everything had gone so horribly wrong. John closed his eyes, Claire's voice sparking memories he'd tried desperately to suppress — late nights reviewing case files, celebrating victories against Dark Wizards, and the way they always had each other's backs.

"Please open up," Claire called again. "I know it's been a long time, but I wouldn't be here if it wasn't vitally important."

John wavered his hand on the door handle. He wanted no reminders of who he used to be before shame and tragedy had claimed him. And yet...this was Claire. Despite his better judgment, he slowly opened the door.

Claire stood on his threshold looking just as he remembered — chestnut hair pulled neatly back, hazel eyes radiating purpose. John froze, the sight of her hitting him harder than expected. It was like looking at a photo of a loved one who died tragically young. Nostalgia, heartache and regret all swirled inside him at once.

"John." Claire's voice cracked with emotion. Up close, he could see the toll the years had taken — faint stress lines around her eyes, a wary sort of hypervigilance. But despite it all, her essence remained the same. Still fighting the good fight when so many others had long given up hope.

Claire shifted on her feet. "I'm sorry to barge in after so long. But time is not on our side. May I come in so we can talk?"

John hesitated, then reluctantly stepped aside. Claire strode past briskly and turned to survey the apartment. He saw her scan the space with the strategic eye of a mage, undoubtedly cataloging details — sparse furnishings, lack of personal effects, his unkempt state. If she judged him for the broken wreck he'd become, her expression hid it well. But then, she had always been enviably disciplined.

"You look well," John lied after an awkward silence. Her answering smile was strained. He cleared his throat, desperate to get this over with. "Why are you here, Claire?"

Her expression turned grim. "I wish this was only a social visit. But as I said, time is not on our side." Claire began pacing as she spoke. "For months, we've been tracking whispers that the Supranium Amulet has resurfaced. Two hours ago, our intel sources reported that followers of Victor have it in their possession."

John's chest tightened involuntarily at the name. He turned away, raking a hand through his disheveled hair. Victor, the warlock, had eluded capture for years. But if his most fanatical devotees now had the Amulet...

"God help us all," John rasped.

"Then you understand why I'm here," Claire said urgently. "Your expertise could mean the difference between salvation and disaster."

John shook his head bitterly. "You

give me too much credit. The man who might have made a difference died a long time ago."

"I don't accept that." Claire's ponytail swished back and forth as she shook her head. "I know you, John Gray. Mage or not, you have never been one to back down when people need you."

John turned away, raking his fingers angrily through his disheveled hair. "You don't understand. I'm done with that life for good."

Unbidden, a vivid flashback ensued... John, years prior, confidently tasked with protecting the Amulet. He felt the cold metal weight of it in his palm, the swirling purple gem mesmerizing yet unsettling. He had sworn an oath to always keep it safe. The memory of how sure he had felt back then cut especially deep. Arrogant fool.

The vision shifted, warping into familiar nightmare fodder. A blast of heat and noise overwhelmed his senses. The

Amulet was ripped away in slow motion as John flew backward. Blood-curdling screams filled the air as calamity erupted all around him. The acrid smell of smoke threatened to suffocate him. Through it all, the crushing despair of failure weighed heavier than any physical pain. He had failed them all.

With a gasp, John wrenched himself back to the dim present. The lingering screams echoed in his head. Rough hands grasped his shoulders, and he lashed out blindly.

"John! It's me, you're safe." Claire's voice sounded far away. He blinked hard, her worried face swimming into view. John pulled away sharply, shame burning through him. Weakness was unpardonable, a dangerous liability.

Claire hovered nearby, radiating compassion. "You've carried the weight of this alone for far too long, haven't you?"

John turned away, struggling to rein in his emotions. He sank into a battered armchair and dropped his head into his hands. "You have no idea how many ghosts haunt me," he said hoarsely. "No idea how profound my failure was that day."

Claire's voice was gentle but relentless. "Perhaps there is more to the story than you realize. The Ministry has reopened the investigation into the disaster. There is strong evidence you may have been made a scapegoat by rivals. Put under impossible expectations by incompetent leaders. Betrayed and blamed unfairly."

John let out a harsh, jagged laugh. "Of course, I was blamed! As I should be. I swore to protect the Amulet with my life, and I failed." He looked up at her with haunted eyes. "Betrayed by rivals or not, the dead still reproach me every night. Their blood stains my hands eternally. No investigation can absolve me of that."

Claire's ponytail swished as she shook her head vehemently. "You judge yourself too harshly. The John Gray I knew was devoted to protecting the vulnerable. A good man who inspired countless others. That man is still in you." She knelt before him, eyes shining with conviction. "If you walk away now, the John Gray I loved and respected will be lost forever."

John turned from her in anguish, bitter laughter choking in his throat. "Your faith is misplaced. That honorable man is long dead. Even if he wasn't, some sins can never be redeemed. The ruins of the life I destroyed are insurmountable."

With a frustrated noise, Claire turned and slapped a stack of case files down on the rickety table. Gruesome crime scene photos spilled out accusingly. "Is this the legacy you want, John? To abandon the innocent while this cursed Amulet leaves more bodies in its wake?"

She stabbed her finger at a photo of a family slain by the Amulet's fire. "These people are dead because of one warlock's obsession. Will you allow their deaths to be in vain?"

Claire grasped John's shoulders fiercely, forcing his gaze upward. "Look at me! That courageous protector is still within you, John Gray. You made mistakes, but your spirit was never broken. Rise up now before more families are ripped apart! Reclaim who you truly are!"

Overwhelmed by her onslaught, John buried his head in his hands once more. The will to fight had been utterly drained from his body and soul long ago. In a ragged whisper, he confessed, "I cannot face the possibility of failure again. It would utterly destroy whatever scrap of my humanity remains."

Something in his confession seemed to deflate Claire. She stepped back, ponytail swishing angrily as she turned toward the door. But there she hesitated, hand poised on the knob. Slowly, she looked back over her shoulder.

"That noble heart does yet beat inside

you. Quietly, perhaps, but persisting still. Don't silence it forever, John." Her voice dropped to a near whisper. "The world needs that light, even if you've lost sight of it inside yourself."

With those enigmatic parting words, she closed the door firmly behind her, leaving John staring after her long after she had gone.

Alone in the dim apartment once more, John slowly raised his tormented gaze to the single personal effect he permitted himself — a faded photo of two young mages on the cracked plaster wall. Their smiles radiated optimism and courage. John stared at that smiling stranger who wore his face. The man who had not yet learned how cruel the fates could be.

"Oh, how I envy your ignorant faith," John whispered to his frozen doppelganger. "Hold onto it dearly as long as you can."

He lowered his face into his hands once more, Claire's impassioned plea echoing through his mind. She had always seen the best in him and believed steadfastly in his inner nobility. But how could John reclaim courage that had been shattered beyond repair? The man who might have risen to this challenge was irrevocably lost.

Or was he? Some small voice inside insisted that a flicker of who he once was yet remained. Faint but refusing to fully be extinguished. Something in him still wanted to make Claire proud, to be the sort of man who did what was right regardless of fear.

John clutched his head, besieged by doubt on all sides. The circles of the past and possibilities of the present collided in his weary mind, sending fractures through his fragile psyche. He squeezed his eyes shut, willing it all away. But the questions Claire's visit had resurrected refused to be silent. They echoed and expanded dangerously, threatening to shake loose demons he had fought so long to contain.

Was redemption only a fantasy?

Or did some small chance at salvation yet remain? John trembled under the weight of it all. In his mind's eye, the ghostly faces swam, equal parts accusatory and hopeful. The nightmares of the past stalked him relentlessly. But so too did Claire's stubborn faith in what he might yet become if only he reclaimed his courage.

John saw once more his younger self in that photograph — full of hope and idealism, unbroken by tragedy or failure. Strong and sure and committed fully to protecting those who could not protect themselves. Had that man truly been lost forever? Or was he merely lying dormant under the layers of guilt and grief that had smothered John's spirit for so long?

He raised his head slowly, daring for the first time in years to really look himself in the eye in that cracked bathroom mirror. Behind the weathered skin and haunted eyes, was that old spark still perceptible? John stared into his own weary soul, searching as he had never allowed himself to before.

There. Barely a flicker. But it was there. Some remnant of who he had been once. And who he might become again if only he could find the courage to reawaken it.

John released a long breath he hadn't realized he was holding. The demons of his past still clung to him, their whispers as sinister as ever. He was afraid, so afraid of making the same mistakes again, of losing himself to darkness and shame as he had these past years. The safer path would be to forever shut the door on Claire's plea.

And yet...John had seen the photos of the Amulet's victims. Innocent lives hung in the balance. If he turned away from them in his fear and self-pity, the John Gray Claire once believed in would be lost forever. This might be his last chance to redeem the man he had been. To take up the torch again, no matter how heavy it had become to bear.

Could he sacrifice what little remained of his hollow existence to protect others?
No. That John had failed.

CHAPTER 3

John woke with a strangulated gasp, pulses pounding in a disoriented panic. The ghosts of his nightmare still clung to him. Their accusing eyes and bone-chilling shrieks echoed in his mind. He squeezed his eyes shut and willed his breathing to slow.

"Just a dream," he rasped into the darkness. "They can't hurt you now."

But the hollow reassurance rang false even to his own ears. The vengeful dead that haunted his sleep were inescapable, their thirst for justice eternal. Or retribution.

With a groan, John hauled himself upright in the sagging bed. Cold sweat plastered his clothes to his clammy skin. His mouth was dry and sour. Sleep had eluded him for hours as it often did these dreary, isolated nights. And when it came, it brought only fresh torments to fray his ravaged psyche.

John rubbed a trembling hand over his stubbled jaw. His fingers caught on the deep grooves grief had carved there. At times like this, consumed by bone-deep exhaustion, the temptation loomed to simply give in. To stop fighting against the relentless darkness and sink into its numbing embrace.

John closed his eyes again, willing his frantic heart to steady. He focused on each breath, in and out until the panicked thrashing in his chest eased. He clung to this simplest proof of life like a drowning man to flotsam. As long as he still drew breath, some flicker of hope endured.

The familiar pre-dawn gloom enveloped the apartment, its shadows deep and monochromatic. John glanced at the window but saw only faint hints of sunrise limning the jagged city skyline. Another interminable day loomed ahead.

With disciplined effort, John swung his legs over the edge of the mattress. His joints creaked in protest, echoing the perpetual weariness that suffused his bones. He ignored their aching pleas for rest. Lingering in this cramped bedroom would only allow the demons to regroup in his mind. Motion and light were the only remedies, however paltry.

The frigid floorboards leeched what little warmth remained from John's feet as he shambled to the bathroom. He winced against the harsh fluorescent lights and dared a glance at his reflection. Haunted, red-rimmed eyes stared back from a face aged well beyond his years. Faint scars and pockmarks marred his sallow skin like an inscription of past battles lost.

With a grimace, John turned away from the stranger in the mirror. He shed his sweat-soaked shirt and splashed icy water on his face and neck until the worst tremors subsided. The meager ablutions helped ground him in the simplicity of physical sensations. Yet they could not wash away the deeper stains on his soul. Those would remain until the end of his days.

John shuffled into the kitchen, shoulders bowed under some invisible weight. Feeble sunlight now filtered through the begrimed window. At least the devils of the night would retreat for a few precious hours.

Out of long habit, John waved his wand to start coffee brewing as he peeled off his sweat-damp pants. The rich aroma cut through the apartment's musty chill. He allowed himself a moment's anticipation of the scalding bitterness. Caffeine's meager stimulations were one of his last remaining pleasures.

As the pot gurgled and hissed, John pulled on faded jeans and an oatmeal pullover. He eyed the threadbare seams critically but shrugged. Vanity held little sway over him these days. So what if he appeared every inch the ruined wretch he felt inside?

Before John could pour his long-awaited coffee, an urgent tapping at the window made him freeze. Apprehension stirred in his gut as he turned to see a large Eurasian eagle owl peering in imperiously. Its amber eyes clearly proclaimed this no mere social visit. Heart sinking, John waved the window open to grant it entry, bracing himself for whatever grim tidings it bore.

The imposing owl fluttered down to perch on a battered bookshelf, its feathers ruffling importantly. Maintaining piercing eye contact, it extended one taloned foot with practiced dignity, revealing an official-looking letter clutched there. John accepted the ominous delivery with a sinking heart. His hands shook slightly as he noted the Ministry seal.

Dread blossomed, cold and suffocating, as John broke the seal and began reading. His worst fears soon bore bitter fruit. Claire was dead. Killed by the same Dark Wizards who had stolen the cursed Supranium Amulet. She had sacrificed herself trying to stop them from unleashing its apocalyptic power.

John's anguished "No!" split the silence like a gunshot. His legs gave out, and he collapsed backward into a chair. Claire dead? Impossible. She had always burned far too bright for something as banal as death to claim her.

But there it was in stark black and white. She had died in pursuit of the fanatics she hunted, refusing to abandon the cause despite the risks. It was so like Claire not to falter with lives at stake, no matter the personal cost. It was the mage code she had upheld right to the end. The code that had defined them both once upon a time.

The letter slid from John's limp fingers as cold reality sank in. Claire was truly gone. Her light had been ruthlessly snuffed out by the very evil they had sworn to combat. And he, broken and defeated, had not been at her side where he belonged.

Raw grief clawed its way up John's throat in a ragged scream. He swayed upright, seized the coffee mug, and hurled it violently against the wall. It shattered on impact, spraying the peeling plaster with bitter liquid.

John gripped the back of the chair as wave after wave of anger and despair crashed over him. "Why, Claire?" He choked. "How could you leave me here alone like this? You were the best of us, the one with all the faith."

No answers came in the dreary little kitchen. Only the unrelenting drip of cooling coffee counted out the passing seconds like the ticking of a clock at a deathbed vigil.

John straightened gradually as the initial wild tempest of his grief spent itself. Jaw clenched, he vanished the mess with a curt wave of his wand. But the external order could not touch the howling chaos Claire's loss had loosed inside him. Its claws would shred his heart until the end of his days.

Moving to the couch on rigid legs, John sank down and dropped his head into his hands. Her death was his fault. Claire had come to him for help to thwart the Dark Wizards and their obsession with the Amulet. She had tried to convince him to fight at her side one last time. But the demons of John's past had long since drained him of conviction. He had been too consumed by shame and self-pity to summon even an ounce of courage.

And so Claire had ventured forth into the darkness alone, never to return. Died because John was too broken and cowardly to stand up when she needed him most. Her blood was on his hands as surely as if he had struck her down himself.

As John hunched there in abject misery, the tap of talons on wood jerked his head up. The solemn owl had not left its perch across the room. It stared at John expectantly, awaiting some response or reciprocation.

"Go away!" John hissed, blinking back hot tears. "I've got nothing to send back."

The owl's unwavering gaze conveyed wordless reproach.

With a snarl, John surged upright and hurled a book at the haughty messenger. "Get out! Nothing can make this right. She's gone, and it's my fault. Now leave me!"

The owl shrieked in protest at this assault but took wing, exiting back through the still-open window into the hazy morning. John slammed the window down viciously in its wake. Then he slumped against the wall as a fresh wave of pain hollowed him out.

By refusing to help Claire when she had humbled herself to ask him, John had signed her death warrant as sure as if he had uttered the Killing Curse himself. No just and loving God could forgive such a sin. Nor should He.

John slid slowly down the wall until he sat with knees drawn up like a child, breath coming in jagged rasps. How could he go on haunted by the look in Claire's eyes if her ghost came to him this very moment? Surely, she would condemn him for the worthless coward he was, a disgrace to the mages and to her memory.

John had no idea how long he sat there numbly, wishing for oblivion before the sound of tapping at the front door roused him. His head jerked up, and pain lanced through his neck from hunching motionless for so long. He blinked hard against the room's afternoon gloom, momentarily confused.

More brisk knocking rattled the door, each rap jarring John like a physical blow. The real world was not content to leave him alone with his incubus yet. It demanded he keep trudging forward through the motions of life despite it all.

With a muted groan, John clambered

to his feet. He shuffled to the door, each step heavier than the last, with the dread of whatever news awaited him now. Bracing himself, John opened the door a crack. An agitated courier stood on the threshold holding a scroll tied with a black ribbon. John's stomach dropped. More death tidings.

"Mr. Gray?" the courier prompted hesitantly.

John nodded curtly.

"Delivery from the Ministry. My condolences for your loss." He held out the scroll almost gingerly as if fearing John might shatter at any moment.

John accepted the scroll without comment and eased the door shut again. He stared down at the ominous black ribbon for a long moment before working up the courage to break the seal.

The letter inside bore only a date, time, and formal script:

The Ministry of Magic invites you to a
memorial service in honor of
CLAIRE VANCE
to be held on Tuesday at sunset
in the Mage Memorial Graveyard

John's hands shook violently now. A surge of nausea forced him to sit down before his legs gave out again. He dropped his head into his hands, the letter crumpling in his white-knuckled grip. Hot tears escaped down his ravaged face.

Even now, with death's gaping maw poised to swallow him, too, he was afraid. Afraid to stand over Claire's grave and witness irrefutable proof that the light had gone out of the world forever. It would make her loss undeniably real. Final.

And if John conjured even a fraction of the courage to meet Claire's parents there, how could he face them knowing he was to blame for their only child's death? Surely, they knew in their bereft hearts that John had failed her when she needed him most.

No, John realized with dawning horror he could not attend this memorial. Not if every eye watching accused him while Claire's coffin sank into the earth. He would gladly follow her down to escape such torment.

A guttural sob clawed its way up John's throat. He tore the letter to pieces in a passion. They drifted around him like macabre confetti, trappings of a celebration long ended. He could not say goodbye. Better to let grief consume him completely behind these walls than to withstand public condemnation for his appalling weakness. Claire's flame had gone out too soon because of him.

Perhaps one day, John would find the courage to leave this miserable apartment again and make the dark pilgrimage to Claire's grave. To beg her forgiveness and water the lifeless ground with his tears. But not yet. The wound was still too raw, exquisitely painful. He would surely open his veins before reaching her plot if he ventured out today.

And so John committed the ultimate cowardly act. He severed himself from Claire forever rather than face her family with heartfelt apologies on his lips. They did not yet realize the depth of his guilt. But if they saw him weeping over her casket, surely they would discern the wretched truth.

Instead, John sat alone in the dimming apartment as Claire's memorial came and went. He stared at nothing while the sun dipped below the dingy horizon. As darkness enfolded the city, John buried his face in his hands. His ragged sobs and the distant wail of sirens chorused through the deepening night, a lament without solace.

The next three days passed in a featureless blur. John left the apartment only once for fire whiskey before stumbling back to nurture his grief anew. He moved ghost-like from couch to bed and back, scarcely eating. Dreams came filled with Claire's contorted face, silently pleading for help he could not provide.

John smashed furniture in anguished rage at the injustice. He overturned chairs and splintered the coffee table, wishing the destruction could somehow make things right. But it only left him bloodied and drained. He cursed his former cowardice that had abandoned Claire to her fate.

When the pain became unbearable, John again resorted to drinking. He gulped whiskey desperately, only to gag and retch it back up as visions of Claire's trusting eyes burned through his mind. The alcohol seared his throat, but could not numb this pain. He hurled the bottle away in impotent fury. How could he go on with her blood on his hands?

Ministry owls came more than once over those bleak days, each bearing the same request — John must help track down the

Amulet to avenge Claire and stop further evil. John scowled bitterly at these missives. Once, he might have leapt into action. But now, paralyzing failure had left him a shell of a man. He simply tossed the letters unopened into the fireplace, watching the parchment blacken and wither. What use was he to anyone now?

As the week dragged on, John made himself tune in to the Wizarding Wireless Network's news, however much he dreaded each grim update. The Dark Wizards had grown bold indeed since claiming Claire's life. They attacked anywhere magical artifacts were kept, unchecked in their quest for more power. John turned the radio off quickly, unwilling to hear the gruesome details or speculation on how many more might die.

Guilt gnawed relentlessly at his soul. He had sent Claire to face such evil with no one at her side. The Dark Wizard leader Victor's sneering face haunted John's mind. Soon, other families would know this terrible grief if someone did not stop these monsters.

But not him. John was certain beyond hope now that he had nothing left to give. Years of trauma and tragedy had sapped what little fortitude he once possessed. Dark magic or drink would claim him long before he found the courage to take up arms as a mage again. And so the death toll rose unabated as John's will crumbled.

When he slept at all now, nightmare visions came of Claire's ghostly pale form hovering at the foot of his bed. She wordlessly implored him to make things right. But she may as well have asked John to single-handedly defeat a dragon. He would disappoint her in the spirit world as profoundly as he had when she lived. All that remained was to let the cold void swallow him, too.

These spectral visitations always jolted John from sleep, shrieking Claire's name. But the dark stillness around him would soon drag his spirit back down to listless depths. He drew his quilt tighter, unable to face the light of duty.

During rare forays out for provisions, John noted the contempt in others' eyes when they recognized him. At the Hag & Hawthorns one night, the surly bartender openly scorned him as a disgrace to the mage title. Other patrons glared in disgust at the ruin of a once-respected man. John didn't argue, just stared into his pint as their judgmental words washed over him. There was no denying what a pathetic coward he had become. He slunk home before drunkenly raging could worsen matters.

Alone again in his dim apartment, John found himself gazing often at the lone personal effect on his barren walls — an old photo of himself and Claire from better days. Their smiles shone with that invincible hope and courage of youth. John traced Claire's face in the photo, his own youthful grin mocking him now. How he envied that John, who had believed himself Claire's brave equal.

John wept bitterly before this relic, this glimpse of a doomed, happier past. "Why couldn't I have your unflagging strength?" He beseeched his frozen image of Claire. He had always clung to her sheer force of will to bolster his own when courage faltered. But now, with only cold ashes left, John felt gutted of all conviction. The hollow man in the mirror was destined only to fail her further.

On the morning a week to the hour after that first mournful letter, another Ministry owl arrived during John's bleary breakfast. This letter bore only four blunt words: Time has nearly expired.

John did not need elaboration. The Dark Wizards must be nearing success in their twisted plots if the Ministry was making a final overture for his help. His throat tightened with grief and frustration.

How desperately he wished events had unfolded differently! That he possessed Claire's selfless courage to offer anything of worth now.

Instead, John simply tossed the urgent letter into the fireplace. He stood motionless, watching the parchment blacken and wither under the flames' indifferent hunger. Only ash remained. Ash was now the sum of his pathetic life as well. Let it blow away on a hollow wind. He had nothing left.

In the sleepless days that followed, John felt himself slipping into true madness. He wandered the apartment at all hours, haggard face twisted in anguish, muttering arguments with the bitter fates over Claire's death. A violent aura seemed to crackle around him. When it burst out, crockery and furniture splintered under the wild force of his magic unleashed.

John took to rising in the dead of night when his nightmares crescendoed, unable to face the specters another moment. He would dress with fumbling hands and stumble out into the chill darkness, walking for hours through sodium-lit streets populated only by thieves and lost souls. He passed unharmed among them like a ghost.

One drizzly night close to dawn found John lumbering up the stairwell of his building in defeat after hours of haunting alleys and empty parks. His shoes squelched on the cracked tiles with every weary step upward. The cold rain had soaked through to his bones but done nothing to quell the tempest within.

He emerged onto the roof, landing in a daze, raindrops pelting his hunched shoulders. Some mad impulse drew John toward the roof's edge. He staggered into the predawn gloom until his legs hit the low parapet wall.

Far below him, the city was lost in mist and shadow. The alleys and rooftops blended into a featureless void. John tilted his head up toward the weeping heavens.

The icy rain needled his skin relentlessly. Even the skies wept over a world gone wrong.

John blinked down into the churning abyss. Would it be such a terrible sin to hasten the inevitable? To spare himself days or weeks more of this ceaseless agony? He had no family left to mourn him. Only the gutted shell of what was once a man remained.

Claire was gone, the virtuous mage calling scrubbed out. And he lacked even the courage to face death with some scrap of dignity intact. Perhaps it would be a mercy to just...tilt forward and let the void rush up to swallow him.

John swayed dangerously, his toes over the ledge. Just one more inch and this anguish could end. His wet clothes slapped the mortar, buffeted by the wind's indifferent hand. John shut his eyes as lightning seared the sky. One more inch and he would fall like Lucifer from grace.

In that suspended moment, John saw Claire's face in his mind once more. Not twisted in rebuke, but radiant and hopeful as he remembered her best. Somehow, he knew she was the one thing tethering him to the world now. He teetered on the precipice between surrender and redemption. But the choice remained his alone, as did the consequences.

With a convulsive gasp, John threw himself back from the lethal ledge, collapsing to hands and knees. He retched violently there as reality returned in a nauseating surge. Had he really nearly committed such ultimate cowardice? Taken the easy way into oblivion and left Claire's death unavenged?

John dragged himself upright and staggered back inside, shame scalding his face. Claire had sacrificed everything for the sake of light, and here he was, ready to plunge deeper into darkness at the first temptation. He truly did not deserve the honor she had shown him once. He scarcely deserved to breathe the same air as one noble as Claire.

But the fact remained — John did still draw breath, however undeservedly. By some twist of fate, he walked while Claire lay cold in the ground. He owed her a debt now that could only be repaid one way — by carrying forth her unfinished work.

The revelation shuddered through John's soul like sunlight breaking through clouds. He had abused the gift of life Claire's death granted him. He saw that now with brutal clarity. Moping in shadows changed nothing. Action did. He had a responsibility to uphold her legacy before this flicker of life went out.

For the first time since the news of Claire's death, John felt the faintest spark of conviction reignite inside his weary soul. The tasks ahead would likely destroy him. He felt woefully unequal to the sacrifices Claire had made. But he must try with her face guiding him.

John entered his apartment just as the rising sun crested the horizon. Its rays reached through the begrimed window to illuminate him with newfound promise. He stood tall as the light bathed his ravaged face. Today was the first day of his atonement. He would either fulfill his duty or die in pursuit of it. But he would not squander Claire's gift of redemption again. That solemn vow now lit his way forward from darkness.

CHAPTER 4

John nursed his whiskey in the dingy corner of the bar, avoiding eye contact with the other seedy patrons. The lighting was dim, shadows gathering in the corners like clustered spider webs. A musty odor of stale beer and body odor permeated the place. The tables were etched with crude carvings of skulls, pentagrams, and other dark symbols.

Raucous laughter made John glance up. A group of three hags cackled as they clinked glowing green shots of vile-looking liquid. Their wrinkled faces were heavily shadowed with makeup, giving them a ghoulish appearance. One had a large facial wart with thick hairs sprouting from it. Another's crooked teeth were blackened and decaying. John winced as their shrill cackles grated on his ears. The rest of the bar's patrons gave the hags a wide berth. Everyone here wanted to avoid attention.

Well, almost everyone. John noticed a young woman sauntering through the tables toward him. She moved with an easy grace, apparently undaunted by the bar's unsavory character. Her embroidered leather jacket, thigh-high boots, and a multitude of clinking bangles marked her as someone who was comfortable in these disreputable circles. An amused half-smile played about her lips as she paused beside John's table.

Up close, he could see she had a heart-shaped face with delicate features framed by long dark hair. But her most striking feature was her intense eyes, which peered at John with unnerving perceptiveness.

"Well, well," she said, "if it isn't the disgraced mage slumming it with the dregs of society."

John tensed at her words, keeping

his eyes fixed on his drink. He willed the woman to move on, leave him to brood in solitude. No such luck. She slid into the chair opposite him, leaning forward on her elbows.

"Most Ministry folk wouldn't set foot in a place like this," she continued. "Not after that business with the Supranium Amulet."

John's insides clenched at the mention of the Amulet. Guilt and shame rose up, threatening to swallow him. He could see it all again — Claire pleading with him to help secure the Amulet...seeing images of her body later, the light gone from her eyes... knowing he was responsible...

With effort, John dragged himself back to the present. The woman's last words lingered in his mind. She knew who he was and about his history with the Amulet. Alarm bells went off in his head.

"Do I know you?" he asked gruffly, finally meeting her disconcertingly direct gaze.

"No, but I know you, John Gray. Former star mage turned reclusive drunk."

John's jaw tightened. It was clear this woman wanted something from him. But what? And how did she know so much about him?

"Who are you?" he demanded. "What do you want?"

The woman's grin broadened, showing very white teeth. She seemed to be enjoying herself immensely.

"People call me Talia," she said, imbuing her name with exaggerated mystery. "Let's just say I trade in information. And right now, I'm betting you need some."

John studied her warily. Traders in illicit information were often untrustworthy types. He would have to be cautious until he knew her angle.

"I don't know what you've heard," John said slowly. "But I think you've got the wrong man. I'm nobody special these days."

He started to rise from his seat, but

quick as a snake, Talia's hand shot out and gripped his wrist tightly. Her playful look had vanished, replaced by one of intent seriousness.

"I wasn't finished," she said sharply.

John hesitated, then sank back down in his chair. Talia released her hold on his wrist, staring at him intently.

"Word is the Amulet's resurfaced," she said. "Powerful forces want to get their hands on it. Could unleash untold havoc across England." She leaned even closer, her gaze boring into him. "But you already knew that...didn't you, John?"

John's breath caught in his throat. Ever since Claire's death, he'd feared the Amulet thieves were active again. This woman — Talia — had just confirmed his worst fears were true. But how could she possibly know about all this?

Seeing his conflicted expression, Talia continued. "Claire recruited you to consult on the investigation. But you refused because of what happened five years ago."

John froze. Those facts weren't public knowledge. Only someone with Ministry connections could know that Claire had approached him about the Amulet.

He studied Talia with new eyes, turning over possibilities. She seemed to genuinely want to help recover the Amulet before disaster struck again. But how had she uncovered such closely guarded details about the case?

"Why should I believe you?" John challenged. "This could be some kind of trap."

Talia sighed impatiently and dug into her jacket pocket. She pulled out a folded newspaper and shoved it across the table to John.

"Page three," she said. "You'll find details about a jewelry store heist last week. Dark Wizard markings were left at the scene."

John scanned the article with a

sinking feeling in his gut. The information here matched Claire's stolen case files. This was no hoax. Cold purposefulness replaced some of John's wariness. Whoever this Talia was, she knew things that could prove vitally important.

"They took a rare diamond," Talia explained, "with unique dark energy containment properties. Essential for handling the Amulet without deadly consequences."

She leaned forward again, holding John's gaze intently. "I move through different circles than the Ministry. Hear things they don't. Uncover secrets. If we're going to find the Amulet first, you need someone who understands this world."

She jabbed a finger at the news article. "I can be your guide, John. But we'll have to act fast."

John sat very still, conflicted emotions warring within him. Tracking down the Amulet would mean confronting the demons of his past. Dragging back to the surface all the bitter shame and self-loathing he had tried to drown in whiskey these past years.

Could he really go through all that again?

"I already failed once," he said bitterly, shoving the paper back toward Talia. "Lost the Amulet. Got my partner killed." His voice dropped to a tortured whisper. "I can't make this right. You need to find help somewhere else."

He started to rise again, but Talia's next words froze him in place.

"So you're fine with the Amulet in the hands of the Dark Wizards?" Anger flashed in her eyes. "Going to sit here drinking while they unleash it on the world?"

John's shoulders hunched defensively. "You think I don't care? That I don't feel responsible?" He glared back at her. "I'll never stop feeling bloody responsible! But I can't do this again. I'm not strong enough this time either."

His voice cracked on the last words. Talia's angry look faded. For a long moment, she just watched his face as he struggled to master himself.

"Sometimes the only way out is through, John," she said eventually, very quietly. "I know it's hard. But burying the past won't erase it. This is your chance to make amends."

John let out a harsh laugh. "You make it sound so straightforward. Like redemption is just waiting out there for the taking." He shook his head bitterly. "After what I've done, there are no second chances."

Talia reached out and gripped his hand tightly until he looked up. Her expression radiated fierce resolve.

"You're wrong," she said. "I know you feel broken right now. But it's never too late to piece yourself together again." Her eyes were intent on him. "We've all made terrible mistakes, John. What counts is finding the courage to face them."

John held her intense gaze, her words striking a chord deep within him. Something in her fervor hinted at personal experience. In that moment, he perceived a kindred spirit in Talia — another seeker looking for meaning in the wreckage of the past.

Could she be right? Was redemption still possible despite the gnawing doubt and self-loathing that consumed him?

Talia seemed to read the conflict on his face. Gently releasing his hand, she said, "I know you're afraid, John. This won't be easy for either of us. But we can make this right if we face it together. What do you say?"

John dropped his eyes to stare into his half-empty glass. Shadows moved across his unshaven face as he wrestled within himself. His gut churned with bitter regret and futility. But Talia's words awoke long-buried flickers of hope. Hope for a future where the shame of his failure no longer weighed so heavily upon him.

Gradually, John became aware of Talia watching him patiently. Her steadfast poise conveyed a deep-rooted belief in second chances. Slowly, John raised his eyes to meet her compassionate yet resolute ones.

Swallowing hard, he gave a single nod.

Talia's serious look vanished, replaced by a triumphant grin. She signaled the bartender, who approached reluctantly, sizing them up with suspicious beady eyes.

"Two Fire whisky shots," Talia told him briskly.

The bartender hesitated, still eyeing them warily. Talia fixed him with an icy stare. "Now."

With a sullen look, the bartender turned to pour their drinks. Talia gave John a satisfied smile. But his earlier doubts resurfaced. There was still so much about her motives that remained uncertain.

Sensing his lingering hesitance, Talia

spoke quietly so only he could hear. "I know you find this hard to believe. But some of us really do want to make the world a little less dark." Her eyes were earnest. "I just need you to have faith, John."

He searched her face and found nothing but sincerity. Before he could reply, the bartender slapped their drinks down and hovered there pointedly.

Talia's gaze locked onto him like a laser. "While you're here, why don't you tell us where your friends have been keeping that diamond they stole last week. The one fenced from that jewelry shop."

The man visibly paled, his eyes darting around nervously. "I got no idea what you mean," he mumbled unconvincingly.

Talia smiled without warmth. "Oh, I think you know exactly what I mean. And where it's hidden currently."

Sweating, the bartender stammered out an address near the docks. Talia nodded, satisfied. The man hurried away, not looking back.

Raising her shot glass, Talia gave John a little salute. "To second chances."

John swallowed his fire whisky in one burning gulp. It seared away some of his doubts, leaving behind a steely purpose. He had wallowed in the shadows long enough. It was time to take a stand.

"Let's do this," he said.

Talia grinned and downed her own shot. As she led the way out of the bar, John felt the heavy weight of the past lift ever so slightly from his shoulders. He drew a deep breath of the cold night air. A sense of hope stirred within him for the first time in years — fragile and tentative but undeniable.

There could be no changing the past. But the future lay ahead of him, its path not yet set in stone.

CHAPTER 5

John stood in the middle of his cramped apartment, staring at the open trunk on the floor. A thin layer of dust coated the once-shiny mage robes folded inside. He reached down and brushed a hand over the familiar fabric, memories rushing back. How long had it been since he donned these robes and ventured out into the streets doing honorable work? Too long, a voice inside whispered. Far too long.

With slow reverence, John lifted out the robes and laid them on a chair. Next came the boots, the wand holster, and the enchanted goggles for seeing magical auras. Each item unleashed a fresh wave of reminiscence—the glory days when he had proudly served as a defender against dark forces. Before everything crumbled apart.

He shook off the lingering bitterness and focused on unpacking the trunk. These tools had gathered dust for too long already. It was time to put them to use again.

John inventoried his other mage artifacts next. The Sneakoscope, pocket-sized but powerful. The Decoy Detonators that could create distracting diversions. And most vital, the stash of ready-to-consume potions. Bottles of Felix Felicis to impart luck. Invigoration Draughts to restore energy. And Calming Draughts for those moments when past shadows overwhelmed him.

As John assembled these vital supplies, he felt his pulse quicken with anticipation. For the first time in forever, he had a purpose again. A chance to correct old mistakes. To make Claire and the others proud.

The thought sent a fresh spasm of grief through him. In his mind's eye, he saw

Claire's face that last time, full of hope that he would help safeguard the Amulet. He had failed her then, but not this time. Not again.

With renewed resolve, John placed the last item gently in the trunk. He straightened up and caught a glimpse of himself in the hall mirror. The face staring back gave him a shock. Haggard and worn, with overgrown stubble and disheveled hair. This would not do. If he wanted the world to see him as a hero reborn, he needed to look the part.

John spent the next hour washing up and making himself presentable again. He trimmed his ragged beard and combed out his tangled hair. Donned a crisp shirt and jacket, the first respectable clothes he'd worn in ages. By the time he cinched his wand holster around his waist, a transformed man gazed back from the mirror. Still worn by grief and regret but with a glint of his old vigor rekindled in his eyes.

John tore his gaze from the mirror.

Time to make it official. Striding to the cluttered desk, he took out a sheet of parchment and quill. The note to the Mage Department was brief but would shock them nonetheless:

I wish to offer my full assistance in securing the Supranium Amulet. Please provide all necessary details on its whereabouts and the last known activities of the dark forces pursuing it. I am ready to make amends for past mistakes. — JG

John read over the parchment once more, then folded it tightly. After today, there would be no turning back. He carried the note to the window, where his tawny owl waited patiently.

"Take this to the Ministry straight away," John instructed as he tied the parchment to its leg. With a gentle hoot, the owl swooped off into the morning sun. John watched it diminish to a speck. His declaration was officially made.

A knock at the door made him turn.

He opened it to find Talia surveying him up and down, eyebrows raised.

"Well, well," she said with a sly smile. "Don't you clean up nicely after all."

John gave a rueful chuckle. "I figured if I'm heading back into the jaws of the Ministry, I should look presentable at least."

Talia's smile faded. She searched his face intently. "This is really happening then? You're ready for this?"

John nodded. "I sent an owl pledging my full help moments ago. There'll be no backing out now." He met her eyes steadily. "I meant what I said last night. It's time I faced my past."

Talia studied him a moment more, and then her face relaxed into a proud smile. "You have no idea how long I've waited to hear you say that." She gripped his shoulder warmly. "We'll get through this, John. Together."

Buoyed by her faith, John donned his mage robes. The enchanted fabric settled comfortably over his shoulders, like the welcoming embrace of an old friend. He fastened his wand sheath around his waist and straightened up tall.

"Let's do this."

The Ministry had not changed much, John noted as he strode down its bustling corridors. The same elaborate tile floors, the flurry of paper airplanes whisking overhead. But instead of smiles and hails of welcome, he now faced turned backs and averted eyes from former colleagues. The word was out already — the disgraced mage had returned.

John squared his shoulders and ignored the sidelong glances. There was only one person's assessment that mattered right now.

The Head Mage's door bore the tarnished plaque: Rufus Castle. John rapped twice sharply, then entered without waiting for a reply.

Castle glanced up from his heavy mahogany desk, face betraying no surprise.

But there was wariness in his eyes as he surveyed John's robes.

"So the rumors were true," he said gruffly. "You've decided to help after all."

"I have," John replied simply.

Castle continued staring at him. "This is your last chance, you know. Mess it up this time, and you're out for good."

John met his gaze levelly. "I appreciate you giving me this opportunity. I know I've forfeited your trust. But I intend to earn it back."

Castle considered him a moment longer before nodding. "Very well. Take a seat."

He spent the next hour briefing John on all the latest details of the Supranium Amulet case. Its destructive powers were even greater than John recalled — capable of laying waste to half of England if unleashed. He listened grimly as Castle described the recent activities pointing to a coordinated effort by forces unknown to secure the

Amulet for their own ends.

A familiar name rang out: Victor Mansfield. John's former partner, Miles' brother, now confirmed to be among those seeking the Amulet. Another specter from his past returned to haunt him. John absorbed it all without flinching. He had expected complications. Ghosts of the past could not deter him any longer.

"These vipers are slippery," Castle concluded. "We've been trying to track their contacts and hideouts without success. You'll need to employ some of your...less conventional methods."

John inclined his head. "I have assistance lined up on that front."

Castle's mouth twisted slightly at the implied association with underworld figures. But he did not protest. Desperate times called for flexible principles.

"I expect you to be back in my office tomorrow. Keep me informed of your progress," was all Castle said. "And Gray...

good luck."

The sentiment, gruffly spoken as it was, stirred John's heart. Perhaps all was not lost here. He still had allies within these walls. All he needed to do was prove himself again.

John spent the remainder of the day preparing for the daunting task ahead. He acquired a fresh owl from the magical creatures emporium to assist communications during his travels. A regal horned owl with intelligent yellow eyes. John sensed a kindred spirit in the bird's steady gaze.

"We have difficult work ahead, my friend," John told it as they exited the shop. "But together, we will prevail." The owl gave a gentle hoot in response.

John's next stop was an old apothecary down Knockturn Alley, where the proprietor asked no questions. He replenished his stock of healing potions and stamina elixirs. His final errand was to revisit his former mage office, now collecting dust. John retrieved a stash of Decoy Detonators and Peruvian Darkness Powder — tools for subtle maneuvering he had mastered long ago.

As he collected these supplies, memories threatened to overwhelm him. Late nights poring over case files with Claire. Deep discussions of vigilance tactics with Miles. John clenched his jaw and focused on the present. There would be time to make peace with the ghosts of this place — but not yet.

Laden with packages, John arrived at the appointed meeting spot in a back corner of the Leaky Cauldron. Talia was waiting in a shadowy booth, sipping a goblet of wine. She had exchanged her leather jacket for dark robes that allowed her to blend seamlessly into the pub's shady atmosphere. A half-smile quirked her lips as John slid into the booth across from her.

"I see you've been busy today," she remarked, eyeing his collection of packages.

"Just getting prepared. I'll need to be ready for anything." John unrolled a map on the table. "Have you made progress tracking our underworld contacts?"

Talia nodded, all business now. "I have a meeting arranged with an informant near the docks tomorrow at sunset. He traffics in illegal magical objects — if anyone knows who's been hunting for the Amulet, it will be him."

She pointed a manicured fingernail at a location on the map. "There's an old warlock in Knockturn Alley who games with some of Victor Mansfield's men regularly. I can win his trust and get invited to their card games. Should provide good intel."

For the next hour, they plotted out a strategy, Talia briefing him on the seedy figures she could leverage for information. John's respect for her cunning grew. However she had come by her unconventional skills, they would prove incredibly valuable in navigating the dark underworld.

As they rolled up the map, John glanced at Talia curiously. "You never did tell me how an upstanding woman like yourself became so experienced with this dangerous lot."

A shadow seemed to pass over Talia's face. She looked away, rearranging the map tubes needlessly. "We all have pasts we're not proud of," she said quietly.

John sensed there were deep wounds beneath the surface, much like his own. But he merely nodded. "I suppose you're right."

Their conversation moved to practical preparations. But John did not miss the subtle hints about Talia's history that suggested a difficult road to her present confidence and poise. Inexplicably, he felt certain their paths had converged now for a reason.

Outside the Leaky Cauldron, John gazed up at the setting sun. Long shadows stretched across the cobblestoned street. His destiny lay somewhere out there in the coming darkness. But with Talia's aid, he would finally make things right.

Squaring his shoulders, John strode purposefully toward the hidden gateway where Talia waited. He stepped through without hesitation, ready to face whatever lay ahead. The ghosts of his past could haunt him no longer.

CHAPTER 6

John strode through the Ministry Atrium, keeping his gaze fixed straight ahead. He could feel the weight of stares and hear the whispers swirling around him. The disgraced mage had returned. After five years of absence and shame, John Gray walked these halls again.

The gossip was only to be expected. John had rehearsed this moment in his mind many times. But the reality still stung. These had been his fellow defenders of the light once. Now, they looked upon him as little more than a traitor.

Only one pair of eyes mattered right now, John reminded himself. Let the others judge all they wanted. He had a job to do.

"Well, look who it is." The scornful

voice of Miles Richmond sliced through the murmurs. "Come crawling back at last, have you?"

John paused, swallowing his instinctive flare of bitterness at the sight of his former partner. Miles looked much the same — tall and broad-shouldered, with a hard edge to his ice-blue eyes. Eyes that were fixed on John with unveiled contempt.

"I didn't come back to crawl," John said evenly. "I came to help end this threat."

Miles stepped closer, his voice dropping to a fierce whisper. "Don't pretend you actually care, Gray. We all know you're just trying to save your pitiful reputation." His lip curled. "But it's too late for that now."

John stood motionless, resisting the urge to lash back. Miles was clearly intent on goading him into a confrontation. John refused to give him the satisfaction.

"If you'll excuse me, I have work to do," he said brusquely, stepping around Miles toward the mage department.

"Don't think I'll make this easy for you!" Miles called after him angrily. "I'll be watching your every step. One toe out of line, and I'll make sure you're out on your ear for good this time!"

John quickened his pace, ignoring the threat. Miles had always been over-competitive, even back in their early training days. His resentment now was no surprise.

As Head Mage Castle's door came into view, John paused to steady himself. That had been merely the first test. There would be far greater challenges to come. But he would face them with courage and patience.

At John's entrance, Castle looked up from the paperwork on his desk, face expressionless. But there was a wariness in his eyes that gave John a pang. Castle had mentored him since his very first day as a bright-eyed young recruit. Had reassured him after John's first failed mission that it only made success sweeter. To see doubt in those familiar eyes now cut deeply.

But John buried the hurt as he took the seat across from Castle. There could be no resentment here if he hoped to regain the trust and respect of the mages.

Castle studied him a moment before speaking. "I'll be frank, Gray. Plenty here think you've got no business being back after the mess you made." His gaze bored into John's. "Convince me that letting you help is not a grave mistake."

John returned Castle's stare unflinchingly. "I understand people's doubts. My failure was costly. But staying away out of shame serves no one."

He leaned forward. "I cannot change the past. But I can damn well help shape the future. What we do now to stop Mansfield and the others will save countless lives."

Castle's expression remained guarded. "I know I told you before you could help again, but the other mages hold no confidence in you. They came to me throughout the day with their complaints that I was giving you another chance. That more may die because you froze when they needed you most. I can't help but think that they may be right. What if they are? What if you crumble when faced with the Amulet again?"

"I won't," John said with quiet certainty. "Whatever it takes, I will finish this."

Castle considered him silently for a long moment. Finally, he gave a curt nod and slid a file across the desk.

"We've had reports of increased dark magic activity down Knockturn Alley. Probably those vipers seeking out cursed artifacts. Look into it."

John accepted the file, pulse quickening. This was his chance to prove himself once more. "I'll report back as soon as I have news."

Castle scrutinized him closely again. "See that you do." He waved his hand in dismissal. "And Gray...tread carefully."

John spent the next several hours renewing old ties among his fellow mages, seeking information on Mansfield's activities. Some, like Kingsley Shacklebolt, greeted him warmly, offering whatever insights they could. But others turned away, muttering, wanting no association with him.

One wizard John approached, Williamson, gave him a look of utter disdain. "Thought you'd left for good, Gray. Shame to see they've let you back in."

John stiffened but kept his tone neutral. "I only wish to help end this threat."

Williamson's lip curled derisively. "Well, you've got a lot of nerve showing your face here again." He turned his back on John and walked away.

John stood very still, fist clenched as he struggled to master the anger and hurt rising within him. He had expected skepticism and mistrust, but the naked loathing in Williamson's eyes rattled him.

Did they all hate him so? John wondered bleakly. Had he truly fallen so far from those golden days when he and his fellow mages were bonded as tightly as family?

No, he told himself firmly. He could not afford to dwell on past camaraderie now. Too much was at stake in the present. He had a job to do. With renewed purpose, John headed for the archives to research Mansfield's known associates. Any scrap could prove the vital missing piece.

The archives room was just as John remembered — shelves laden with case files and magical artifacts, the scent of parchment and dust hovering in the air. He ran his fingers over the neatly labeled boxes chronicling history's greatest Dark Wizard takedowns. A sense of bittersweet nostalgia washed over him. How many hours had he spent here reviewing cases, preparing for missions that kept the world safe?

One box in particular drew John's

eye: August 12, 1998 — Destruction of the Desecrator Cult. That had been John's first big case, just a year out of training. He vividly recalled the satisfaction of tracking down the sinister cult's leaders and bringing them to justice. It had been a turning point, proving his talent and cementing his status as a rising star.

With a pang, John turned away from the box. He could not afford to linger in the past now, no matter how golden it seemed. The present was all that mattered.

Hours passed in a blur as John pored over documents seeking leads. He was so absorbed that the sound of the door banging open jolted him violently. Spinning around, his wand at the ready, John saw Miles glowering at him from the doorway.

"What do you think you're doing in here?" Miles demanded, striding forward.

John straightened up slowly from his crouched position over the archives. "Research. Same as you, I expect."

Miles stopped just inches from him, looming over John threateningly. "I see what this little charade of yours is really about. Trying to wheedle your way back into everyone's good graces." His eyes were cold as stone. "I won't let it happen."

John met his hostility head-on. "Your opinion of me is your own business. But nothing will stop me from completing this mission."

Miles shook his head. "When are you going to get it through your thick skull that you're done here? You're a disgrace to the whole mage department!"

He jabbed his finger painfully into John's chest. "Stay the hell out of my way, you backstabbing traitor. This is your last warning."

With that, Miles spun on his heel and stalked out, slamming the door behind him. John remained frozen for a long moment, his heart pounding. He closed his eyes and took a slow, deep breath, willing his emotions back under control.

Miles' vicious words stirred up a storm inside him. But John refused to let it show. He could endure the contempt and doubt. The stakes were too high now for pride or anger.

Squaring his shoulders, John returned to his research. Another test passed. Miles would keep trying to provoke him, but John would meet it with patience and resolve. That was the only way to prove himself worthy once more.

Over the next week, John pursued every lead connected to the Amulet's whereabouts. He frequented the seedy taverns and shops of Knockturn Alley, where the Mansfield syndicate's goons were known to gather. Even made the dreaded journey out to Azkaban Prison to interview Dark Wizards, who might know something.

The island fortress was just as bleak and bone-chilling as John recalled. The prisoners leered and made crude remarks as he passed their cells. But John kept his composure. He had a job to do.

One emaciated inmate spit at John's feet as he stopped at his cell. Scabior — a former snatcher who had evaded justice for years after the war. John had finally tracked him down five years ago. The sneering prisoner clearly remembered.

"Look who's come crawlin' back," Scabior jeered. "The great Mage Gray, reduced to beggin' scum like us for help." He cackled wildly. "How the mighty have fallen!"

John ignored the taunt. "What do you know about the Amulet's whereabouts?" he asked brusquely. "Or Mansfield's plans to retrieve it?"

Scabior just kept laughing. "Come closer, and maybe I'll tell you. If you dare..."

His snakelike leer sent a chill down John's spine. With an effort, he met the sunken eyes steadily. After a moment, Scabior shrugged.

"I know nothin' about your trinket. But I'll be waitin' for you..." His lips peeled back from rotting teeth. "We all will."

John clenched his jaw and walked on, the eerie laughter echoing down the stone corridor after him. Azkaban held only ghosts now, haunting reminders of the past. No answers waited here.

Late at night, John lay awake going over case notes, searching for any clue he might have overlooked. But exhaustion blurred the words on the page. Blearily rubbing his eyes, he glanced at the bedside clock — 3:24 a.m. He should try to sleep.

Instead, he found himself rereading the eyewitness account of the Amulet's destruction five years ago. The description of its searing purple flame reducing Diagon Alley to ashes triggered a vivid memory. John was there again, trying in vain to shield his face from the blistering heat as buildings crumbled around him. Screams and smoke filled the air. Out of the flames lunged a monstrous shadow...

With a gasp, John snapped the file shut and sat up, heart hammering. For several minutes, he just focused on steadying his breathing. Even now, the memories tormented him. He could not fully outrun the ghosts of his failure.

But he refused to surrender to them. Splashing cold water on his face, John squared his shoulders and looked at his haggard reflection. The past was done. All that mattered now was finding the Amulet again before disaster struck.

John had nearly put the horrific visions from his mind when a new test arrived the next morning. The regal horned owl he had adopted as his messenger dropped an envelope on his table before alighting on the perch by the window.

The letter was addressed in an achingly familiar neat script: Marissa Gray. John's hand trembled slightly as he opened it. The message was brief:

John —

Word has reached me that you have returned to the mages in vain hopes of redeeming yourself. I cannot bear to watch you fail again. The shame is too much. Do not contact me. Just let this go before it destroys what little dignity you have left.

Marissa

John slowly lowered the letter, grief and anger churning inside him. Marissa had been the light of his life once. To receive such a cold dismissal cut him to the bone.

Bitterly, he wondered if she was right. Perhaps this quest would only end in more disgrace and heartbreak. How could he hope to succeed now when he had failed so utterly before?

As the doubts threatened to overwhelm him, John glanced up. His gaze landed on an old photo of himself and Marissa on their wedding day. They were beaming, blissful in their love and hope for the future. The man in that photo would never have surrendered so easily.

John set his jaw, anger hardening into resolve. Marissa had given up on him, but he would not give up on himself. Each hurt and setback only strengthened his commitment. He would see this through to the end.

Setting the letter aside, John donned his mage robes. Time to get back to work.

Late one night, after poring fruitlessly over stacks of Amulet case files, John finally succumbed to exhaustion and collapsed into bed. But sleep brought little respite.

Flames engulfed his dreams once more. The Amulet lay before him, pulsing with malevolent purple light. John reached for it, but searing heat scorched his hands. He tried to run, but his legs stuck fast. Smoke closed in, choking him. The flames leapt higher, taking on a monstrous shape with burning eyes...

With a strangled yell, John bolted upright in bed, sheets tangled around him.

His skin was slick with cold sweat, his heart hammering wildly. For several long minutes, he just focused on taking deep breaths until the lingering visions released their viselike grip on him.

These nightmares were his deepest shame, though he confided them to no one. Even after five long years, John still relived that horrific day in his darkest dreams. They served as an ever-present reminder of his failures.

Once the tremors had passed, John rose unsteadily from the bed. He shuffled into the bathroom and splashed frigid water on his face, then forced himself to meet his own haunted eyes in the mirror.

You cannot hide from this forever, he told himself. The only way forward is through.

Squaring his shoulders, John walked back out into the main room with measured steps. A pale pre-dawn light filtered through the curtains. He had a few hours yet before meeting Talia to follow up on a promising new lead.

Sitting at the table, John mechanically began reviewing his case notes again. But the words blurred meaninglessly before his exhausted, burning eyes.

Abruptly, he tossed the file aside and dropped his head into his hands. He pressed his palms against his eyes until colorful dots swam in the darkness. The questions that had plagued him from the start echoed again in his mind:

What made him think he could succeed this time when he had failed so utterly before? Why couldn't he just let it go? Forget the past and live out the rest of his days in obscurity?

As soon as the doubts arose, John rejected them. He knew why he had to see this through, no matter the personal cost. For those who had lost their lives. Those who would be lost if the Amulet resurfaced. And for himself—to reclaim the man he once was.

Renewed conviction flowed through John, washing away the bitter taste of failure. He had fallen many times on this path and would likely fall again. But he would pick himself back up each time, stronger and wiser for it. The long road stretched out before him, but he would walk it unflinchingly to the end.

John arrived early at the meeting point near the docks. In the quiet moments before Talia appeared, he gazed out at the gray river water, lapping gently at the pylons. Its eternal murmuring soothed his lingering unrest. He drew strength from the water's patient, unceasing flow.

This journey was his river. There would be treacherous rapids and obstructing debris ahead. But he would follow it steadily to the sea, correcting his course where needed, never losing faith. And one day, he would emerge into the open waters under a sunny sky, his destination reached at last.

Squaring his shoulders, John turned to greet Talia as she approached. He was ready for whatever lay ahead.

CHAPTER 7

John traced his finger along the ancient sea chart, following the scattered chain of islands until he reached the small one marked only with a skull symbol. He and Talia had spent weeks pursuing whispers and myths about the Amulet's location. All the fragmented clues pointed here — to this remote and notorious island.

"The Isle of Exiles," Talia confirmed, frowning over John's shoulder. "Those banished from proper magical society end up there. Smugglers, thieves, mercenaries — anyone running from the law."

She tapped the skull symbol grimly. "They say only the most ruthless survive there long."

John nodded slowly, already lost in

thought planning their approach. The Isle's infamy would make access difficult, but he refused to be deterred. Not when this was the closest they had come to a solid lead yet. After months of fruitless searching, the possibility of finally achieving his goal thrummed through John's veins. He could almost feel the cursed Amulet within his grasp.

"We'll need a discreet way in," he mused. "A smuggler willing to pose as traders..."

"Leave that to me," Talia said with a sly smile. "I still have certain contacts from my...past life."

John quirked an eyebrow at this oblique reference to her mysterious history but simply nodded. When Talia had first appeared promising help, he had suspected deception. But the months since had proven her loyalty beyond doubt. Whatever secrets lay buried in her past, he trusted her completely now.

"I knew I recruited the right partner in crime," he said.

Talia's smile widened at the compliment. She rose and donned her traveling cloak. "Be ready to leave at dusk. I'll handle the rest."

John spent the intervening hours preparing for their infiltration of the lawless isle. He carefully checked his wand, sharpening it to a fine point, and strapped on his mage dagger — goblin-forged steel. His potions kit was fully stocked with medicinal tonics and toxins to cloud enemies' minds or strengthen his own. And he cleaned his enchanted seeing glass, which enabled sight through solid objects — an invaluable aid for stealth.

Satisfied he was ready for any threat, John made his way as darkness fell to the appointed seaside rendezvous point — a small, deserted cove. The only sound was the hypnotic lap of waves against rock. High above, seagulls circled and called mournfully. A fitting dirge for a voyage to the damned Isle, John mused grimly.

He tensed as footsteps approached from behind. But it was only Talia, accompanied by a grizzled, weather-beaten old sailor. His wrinkled face looked tough as old leather, weathered by decades of harsh sea winds. A curved dagger hung from his belt next to a flask of rum.

"John, meet Captain Rask," said Talia. "He's agreed to smuggle us to the Isle aboard his ship."

The captain spat on the sand. "Normally, I steer clear of that accursed place. But for the right price..." He eyed John and Talia shrewdly.

"We'll triple your usual rate," John said without hesitation. The Ministry's coffers funded this mission; gold was no object. And if this dodgy mariner could get them to the island unseen, it would be cheap.

The captain grinned, displaying an

absence of teeth and gaps in the ruddy gums. "Then let's be off."

They followed him down the moonlit beach to where a battered old skiff was pulled up on the sand. Patches covered holes in the sail, and barnacles encrusted the bow, but the vessel had a sturdy look. John and Talia climbed gingerly aboard, the deck creaking under their weight, while the captain untethered the boat from its stakes. The sail caught the brisk wind with a snap as they turned toward the open sea.

The skiff skimmed over the dark waves, its weathered boards groaning. Spray misted John's face, the salty tang invigorating. In the distance, the Isle of Exiles loomed ever closer. Even from afar, John could make out the fortress carved into its sheer cliffs. Torches flickered along the imposing ramparts, and he thought he heard raucous laughter drifting over the wind — the Isle's damned inhabitants reveling in their lawlessness. John shivered, though not just from the chill wind. That place emanated menace. This would be no simple task.

Sensing his unease, Talia moved closer so only he could hear over the crash of waves. "We've got this, John," she said firmly. "Look how far we've come already."

John nodded, taking strength from her steadfast poise. She was right — together, they had navigated countless dangers since beginning this journey. He would not falter now when answers were almost within reach. The Amulet's siren song pulsed in his veins, inexorable as the tide.

The moon sank below the horizon as they drew nearer the island. "Best to approach hidden under cover of darkness," Captain Rask advised. "The watchers will harpoon any ship that sails openly into the harbor."

John's pulse spiked as the skiff slid through the inky water toward a narrow cave mouth at the base of the cliffs. This was the Isle's smuggler entrance — a gaping maw waiting to swallow them into its corrupt heart. But his hand was steady on his concealed wand. He was ready for whatever lay within that ominous fortress.

The skiff scraped softly onto a strip of stone beach deep in the cave. Dripping stalactites glistened above them. "I'll return in three nights to collect any who still breathe," the captain whispered. "Any longer than that, you're on your own."

John gripped his shoulder briefly in thanks before he and Talia stole off down a rough-hewn passage, leaving the captain shrouded by the boat's dark sail. John felt a twinge of doubt watching Rask's grim face retreat — would they ever reemerge from this godforsaken place? But he shook off the weakness. There was no turning back now.

The passage twisted erratically, seeming to double back and split randomly. But John kept his bearings. At last, it opened up into a vast network of tunnels and chambers carved from the island's heart. Even this late, the caverns seethed with activity. Rough, dangerous-looking characters loitered along the walkways, smoking strangely-colored pipes or playing cards by dim candlelight. Many were disfigured — missing eyes, warped limbs, weapons in place of hands. All eyed John and Talia suspiciously as they navigated the narrow stone walkways.

John's fingers twitched near his concealed wand, senses hyper-alert for any threat. He knew they must seem ripe targets — wide-eyed newcomers in this nest of vipers.

Sensing his caution, Talia murmured, "Let me do the talking. Some here know me from past dealings."

True to her word, she guided them confidently through the labyrinthine underworld. John kept his face impassive, letting Talia take the lead, interacting though his eyes constantly scanned for danger. No one made a move against them, but hostility simmered in the air.

In a shadowy tavern carved right into the rock wall, Talia conversed casually with a battle-scarred group John guessed were mercenaries from the curved blades at their sides. Coins changed hands subtly under the table, and then one beckoned them over to a secluded corner table.

"You seek the Burning Stone, yes?" the man rasped in a hushed tone. His face was a mass of knotted scars. "Many covet its great power. But only the Black Hands control it now."

John leaned intently across the table, pulse racing. The Burning Stone was one of the Amulet's mythic names — it had to be. They were on the right track.

For the next hour, Talia worked her way methodically through the island's network of informants, buying vital tidbits with gold and veiled threats. Bit by bit, the full picture emerged. A ruthless gang called the Black Hands had seized the Amulet during a bloody raid on the mainland. Their headquarters was somewhere deep in the island's tunnels. Now, they sought a way to tap into the Amulet's legendary power — said to magnify magic tenfold for good or evil.

John listened intently to every detail, piecing together the puzzle. The Black Hands clearly planned to abuse the Amulet's might for their own ends. He could not let that happen. The one-eyed fishmonger Talia interrogated next, fingered an engraved rune on his stall. "You'll find their lair by following the Mark of the Serpent." He tapped the rune meaningfully.

John's eyes narrowed as he studied the crude carving — two entwined snakes. This was the vital clue needed to reach the Amulet. If they followed the Mark of the Serpent, it would lead them right to the gang's inner sanctum. The confrontation John had both craved and dreaded since this journey started loomed close at hand.

Back in the twisting tunnels, John lit his wand to search for any similar runes carved into the rock. The passages turned and forked endlessly, but John navigated them with care, following each serpentine Mark that promised to bring them closer to the center. He could almost feel the Amulet calling him onward like a siren's song.

Abruptly, Talia seized his shoulder, yanking John back sharply. He stumbled, then saw the hulking creature lurking just around the bend they had been about to turn — a massive troll, small eyes glinting with malice. Talia gestured at a pile of cracked bones nearby, warning of the predator's proximity. They must have strayed near its lair.

Wand raised, John considered options for dealing with the troll before them without raising an alarm. But there was no time to strategize — with a bellow, the troll charged down the passage toward them. Thinking fast, John cast a hasty Disillusionment Charm, causing them to blend into the rock wall. The troll barreled past, swiping at the empty air. John held his breath until the creature lumbered off down the tunnel, still searching for its vanished prey.

"That was close," Talia breathed. John nodded, mopping sweat from his brow. The tunnels held endless dangers — they would need to be even more vigilant. He set out again, moving swiftly toward their prize. The Mark of the Serpent would guide their way if he kept faith.

At last, the passage widened into an immense cavern with a vast underground lake. Black water lapped at a shore of jagged rocks. Phosphorescent algae on the distant ceiling cast an eerie glow. And on the far side rose a tower of stone that could only be the Black Hands' lair — the Mark was carved prominently above its entrance.

John took a bracing breath as he studied the sinister structure across the dark lake. This was it — the proverbial dragon's den. Somewhere within lay the Amulet, he felt certain. But also great peril if even half the vile rumors held true. His moment of destiny had come at last.

Sensing his hesitation, Talia gripped his hand tightly. "We're so close to answers now," she reminded him gently. "I know the last stretch is the hardest. But we will face whatever comes together."

John squeezed her hand gratefully. Her resolute poise anchored him against his creeping doubts. She was right — they could not turn back when the finish line was in sight. He had conquered demons without and within to reach this point. He would not falter now.

Talia rummaged in her pack for waterproof elixirs while John removed his heavy cloak and boots. They would have to swim the frigid subterranean lake to achieve the tower. John could not suppress a shiver as he waded into the dark water. Its icy chill cut to his very bones. Something brushed his leg, and he stumbled back in alarm before realizing it was only tangled weeds.

Keep your head, he told himself firmly. There were sure to be real dangers ahead. He would need all his courage and cunning.

He had made it halfway across the lake when the still surface exploded around him. Grindylows — foul-horned water demons — burst from the depths to attack. They seized John's limbs with spindly clawed fingers, dragging him under. He thrashed violently, casting a nonverbal Incendio spell. The scalding bubbles provided just enough distraction to tear free of their hold and surge back up, gasping for precious air again.

But the grindylows had tasted blood now. They swarmed toward John just below the surface, eyes glinting with predatory hunger, ready to rend his flesh. Jaw clenched, he spun in the water to face the beasts. If he failed here, all was lost — the Amulet would remain in evil hands.

The lives depending on him flashed before John's eyes, steeling his resolve. With a primal roar, he unleashed a torrent of fire from his wand, scorching the grindylows into retreating into the murky depths. Their shrieks echoed off the cavern walls.

Panting with effort, John staggered onto the rocky shore. His soaked clothes clung to him, the icy water still chilling him to his core. But triumph blazed within him, larger than the doubts that had plagued him for so long. He had conquered his own weaknesses and these monsters. Nothing would stop him now from finishing what he had started.

After helping a shaken Talia onto the shore, John led the way toward the tower's entrance. Inside lay the final leg of this harrowing journey — where light and dark would meet for a final reckoning. As they crept down the dim passage, John could almost feel the Amulet calling to him. Its siren song resonated in his bones, full of promise and temptation. Strange symbols marked the walls, pulsing with crimson light, seeming to writhe and come alive. He kept his eyes straight ahead. There would be time to decipher their meaning when this was finished.

At last, the passage opened into a vast chamber with a soaring ceiling lost in shadow. The stale air was heavy with ominous power. At the chamber's heart sat a stone altar — and atop it, the unmistakable Amulet. Even from afar, John could see it throbbing with otherworldly purple light, beckoning them closer.

John and Talia exchanged an electrified look. The end of their long quest was finally at hand. Together, they stepped into the chamber, wands drawn, ready to face whatever final dangers awaited within.

CHAPTER 8

John and Talia crept forward down the dim stone corridor, wands drawn. Grotesque gargoyles leered at them from alcoves as they passed, and John could have sworn their shadowy eyes blinked and followed them. The walls were etched with arcane runes that seemed to writhe in the flickering torchlight. Dark magic permeated this place — John could feel it like a cold slithering against his mind.

Up ahead, the passage widened into a vast chamber lit by candles made from blackened bone. Strange relics glinted on pedestals — knives crusted in ancient blood, shrunken heads with mouths frozen in screams, a jeweled crown still attached to mottled flesh and hair.

John's senses strained for any sign of guards. But the rooms appeared deserted. Only his and Talia's soft footsteps echoed eerily through the shadows. The Amulet's siren song tugged at John's mind, drawing him onward.

Too easy, he thought. His battle-honed instincts screamed that this was a trap. But they had no choice but to spring it. The Amulet lay ahead. He could feel its seductive dark energy throbbing in his bones.

At a branching of the corridors, John gestured for Talia to take a left while he went right. Better to divide any ambush. She nodded, young face grimly determined beneath her hood. They had survived many trials together already. But John sensed their greatest test lay ahead.

As John crept forward, wand raised offensively, his thoughts inevitably drifted to the past. How easily Victor had swayed him, preyed upon his naivete. John had paid the price for that foolish trust, but so many others had lost far more. The pain and destruction unleashed haunted his nightmares even now. Would he fail again? Had the past broken something within him permanently?

No, John told himself firmly, forcing the doubts aside. He could not change yesterday. But he would face the present with wisdom hard-won.

There, up ahead — John's sharpened senses detected a tripwire shimmering across the passage. A trap, just as he'd suspected. Carefully levitating over the wire, John continued forward, senses tingling. The final confrontation was close now. He could taste it in the brackish air.

Abruptly, a scream rang out from Talia's direction — the tripwire! Then bells clanged deafeningly as the entire corridor erupted into chaos. The trap had been sprung.

John raced back toward the sound,

ducking curses streaking from hidden side passages. Black-cloaked figures closed in on Talia, who stood her ground courageously, blasting them back with powerful countercurses. But too many appeared, forcing her to retreat.

With a slash of his wand, John cleared her a path. "Come on!" he shouted. But a mass of enemies blocked their escape route. They were surrounded and drastically outnumbered. Rough hands wrenched away John's wand before binding his wrists in cursed ropes that bit his flesh. Beside him, Talia, too, was quickly disarmed and restrained. They exchanged an agonized look. After coming so far and surviving such horrors, to fail at the final hurdle was a bitter draught indeed.

A slow, mocking clap echoed from the corridor's end. Victor Mansfield emerged from the shadows, surveying his captives with a cruel smile. The years had hardened his arrogant features. His ice-blue eyes were colder and more cunning than John recalled. Power and madness lurked in their depths. This was a man who had delved too deeply into magic's shadowed recesses.

"Well done on making it this far, John," Victor sneered. "But did you really think you could sneak up on me undetected in my own stronghold?"

John jerked against his bonds, rage and shame flooding through him at the sight of his smirking nemesis. The man who had nearly destroyed him. "I don't fear you, Mansfield," he spat defiantly.

Victor's smile only widened. He traced a contemplative finger down his bone-white wand. "I expected no less stubborn foolishness from you. You never did know when you were outmatched."

His icy eyes bored into John's. "But not even you can undo the past. If only you had surrendered the Amulet when I asked all those years ago, we could have avoided such unpleasantness."

John strained furiously at his ropes, the wounds of his failure ripped open again. "You lied to me! Manipulated my trust to further your own evil."

Victor shrugged. "The righteous are so easily exploited. But you have only yourself to blame this time."

He lowered his face to John's, grinning viciously. "How many died that day in Diagon, John? Because you lacked the fortitude to wield real power when it mattered most?"

With a primal roar, John snapped his cursed bonds through sheer fury and lunged at Victor's throat. But an invisible force slammed him back against the wall, pinned there by dark magic.

Victor watched John's struggles dispassionately, all traces of mirth gone. "I see containment will be necessary with you." He raised his bone-white wand over John's heart. "For all our sakes."

John glared back defiantly, refusing to

show fear. He had known this confrontation might end in death. If so, he would leave this world with honor. Some fates were worse than death. He prayed Talia might still escape to continue their struggle.

Suddenly, Talia shouted a concussive spell, blasting back Victor's guards in an explosion of light. In the confusion, she tossed something small and metal toward John. It bounced and clinked on the stone near his feet — a lock pick.

As Talia grappled fiercely with the disoriented guards, John strained every sinew to reach the pick, the invisible bonds digging into his wrists and shoulders, resisting his efforts. But the struggling Talia's bravery fueled him. He would not fail her courage with weakness. With a primal growl, he broke partly free and grasped the pick, then sprang at the Dark Wizard who had eluded justice for so long. He held out his hand and summoned his wand. It flew into his waiting grasp.

Victor's look of shock quickly hardened into cunning resolve. He slashed his wand with blinding speed, meeting John's barrage of spells with redoubled fury. The stone walls trembled from the force of their immense power. Two master wizards locked in a duel to the death. No more pretense or deception remained between them — only primal will pitted against will.

"You always were the weak one, John," Victor spat, deflecting his attacks almost lazily. "The Amulet knows only the ruthless deserve its gifts."

Chanting in a forgotten tongue, Victor conjured a roaring dragon of shadow and flame. Stone cracked beneath its smoldering claws as the monstrous beast bore down on John. He barely managed to dissipate it with a blast of argent light, rolling away singed.

John fought on relentlessly, summoning every ounce of skill and power. But Victor drew on the Amulet's dark energy to amplify his attacks. Soon, John was driven back, battered and burned. With a blast like a cannon, Victor sent John's wand spinning from his grip. A second invisible blow struck his chest like a sledgehammer, knocking John to his knees with bone-cracking force, the ancient stone slabs cratering beneath him.

Bleeding and overwhelmed with pain, John could only glare up at Victor's sneering face as the dark mage leveled his wand at him in triumph. The faces of all who had suffered swam before John's eyes — he had failed them again. After coming so far, he would die a broken man, as Victor wished. The past could never be outrun.

As despair threatened to engulf him, John's gaze fell on Talia's motionless form. She had sacrificed everything to bring them here, never losing faith in him even through his own doubts. Could he surrender while breath and hope remained?

No! John had sworn an oath as a mage to keep fighting, no matter the odds.

He called on that iron will now, pushing past the agony. There was always hope if he could find the strength to see it.

Digging deep within himself, John drew up his last dregs of power into a potent Shield Charm. Victor momentarily staggered back, caught off guard. In those few seconds, John spotted a heavy black iron torch sconce and blasted it toward the Amulet with the last of his strength. The metal crunched through the relic's crystalline casing, interrupting its flow of power.

Victor howled in rage, lashing out with his wand blindly. But John was already moving, rolling behind pillars and using the environment against his foe. He blasted flaming torches from the walls to create concealing smoke. Toppled marble statues to block curses. Scrambled up shard-lined walls beyond Victor's reach, opening up narrow gaps to return attacks when he could.

Piece by piece, John stripped away Victor's advantages. Separated from the Amulet amplifying him, the man was mortal after all. John ignored the screaming exhaustion of his body and delved deep into his mage skills and training, so long forgotten. He would hold nothing back — this ended now.

As Victor thrashed below in futile fury, John recalled one of the first tactics he had ever learned. With a piercing cry, he drew down lightning from the ether into his fingertips and hurled it at the Amulet shards near Victor's feet. The resulting explosion flung the Dark Wizard across the hall, critically weakened.

Panting with effort, John leapt down and strode over to where Victor lay crumpled. He placed a boot on Victor's chest, pinning him down. The man who had haunted his nightmares now lay broken at his feet. John peered down upon him with more pity than hatred. The past could no longer touch him.

"You will answer for what you've done," John intoned calmly. "There is always a reckoning, Victor. For all our choices."

He bound the defeated wizard in eldritch chains before finally rushing to help the injured Talia to her feet. Together, they turned to gaze upon the Amulet, finally in the right hands. John sighed deeply, feeling the heavy darkness within him dissolve at last. He had faced his demons without and within — and prevailed. The long road had led him back to the light.

CHAPTER 9

As John apprehended the defeated Victor Mansfield, binding the Dark Wizard's hands, a slow, sinister chuckle emanated from the captive man. John paused, a chill running down his spine at the sound.

Victor raised his head, eyes glinting malevolently. "Did you truly think it would be so easy?" he sneered.

Before John could react, Victor's form dissipated into curling black smoke. The echo of his laugh lingered eerily in the chamber. It had only been a conjured projection — the real Victor had never been here at all.

Cursing bitterly, John rushed to where the Amulet had lain. But the altar stood empty, save for scattered shards. The prize he had sacrificed so much for was gone, as was his enemy. Victor had spun a deadly illusion, keeping himself and the Amulet safely out of reach.

John sank to his knees before the desecrated altar, anguish and despair threatening to swallow him. After endless trials and sacrifices, to fail again when success was within grasp was a bitter draught indeed.

Talia appeared at his side, wincing as she nursed her wounded arm. "We will reclaim it," she insisted, voice steady despite her pain. "This is a setback, not an end."

John could not answer, tormented by his mistake. He should have known better. Victor had always been ten steps ahead, anticipating his every move. What made him think this time would be any different? After so many years of failure and fear, he was still the same inadequate fool.

Talia knelt and turned John's face toward her own. "You did everything you could," she said firmly. "No one can predict

Victor's trickery. What matters now is how we respond."

John searched her eyes, clinging to the steadfast faith he saw there. Slowly, her words penetrated the fog of despair enshrouding him. She was right — wallowing in self-pity would not regain the Amulet. John drew a shaking breath and forced himself to analyze the situation rationally, as a mage should.

The intricate ritual artifacts, ancient tomes, and astronomical charts left behind indicated Victor had developed powerful new ways to channel the Amulet's arcane energies and awaken its full destructive potential. Even now, the Dark Wizard could be completing his wicked designs to subjugate all magical society. Time was running short.

"We have to stop Victor before he fully unlocks the Amulet," John said grimly. Talia watched him intently as he began gathering the materials Victor had abandoned. "And that will require fighting fire with fire. I must master the Amulet myself."

As he voiced the awful truth that had been growing within him, John's gut twisted with dread. Was he even capable of wielding such primordial power? He had avoided it for so long, fearful of the devastation he might unleash again...

Talia looked startled, then deeply concerned. "Its power is volatile," she warned. "We've seen the destruction it can unleash." She touched the fresh curse scar on her shoulder with a wince. "There must be some other way."

"There isn't," John said bleakly. "Victor's power is too great already. I am the only one who might withstand the Amulet long enough to undo his schemes."

John turned away, hating the admission hovering on his lips — that he was terrified of the Amulet's seductive power. Always had been. He lacked the fortitude for such forces. But how could he confess this weakness when the world needed him to be strong?

Talia came close and gently turned John to face her again. Her eyes were filled with compassion. "Your caution was wise," she said softly. "Only the most arrogant or deranged would seek to wield such magic lightly." She gripped his hands tightly. "I do not doubt your strength, John. But harnessing such forces leaves wounds that cannot be seen."

John clung to her hands like a lifeline, drawing courage from her steadfast faith in him. Talia had stood stalwartly by his side through endless trials already. Without her guiding light, John knew he would have faltered long ago.

"I am afraid," he confessed at last, hating the shameful words but unable to hold them back any longer. "Afraid I lack the power...the will..." His voice failed him.

Talia squeezed his hands harder. "Yet you have overcome so much already," she reminded him. "You have walked through fire and shadow, conquered enemies without and within." She touched his face gently. "Have faith in yourself, John. In who you have become."

John covered her hand with his own, letting her words sink into his battered spirit, soothing the gnawing self-doubt. When he finally spoke, his voice was steady again. "Stay near, but I must face the Amulet alone." He set his jaw with renewed resolve. "Whatever the cost."

Over the next several days, John immersed himself in arduous study and preparation for the harrowing confrontation ahead. He pored over the ancient tomes Victor had left behind, slowly piecing together the obscure rituals and incantations needed to channel the Amulet's volatile magic without being destroyed by it in turn.

Feverishly, he sought some key, some truth he had missed that would allow him to bend the wild forces to his will. The missing fragment of understanding that had eluded him disastrously once before.

The dusty pages offered fragmentary insights — dire warnings against presumption, shadowed references to the "dual fires" contained within the stone. But no clear pathway to mastering its untamed power.

Only through focusing his mind completely could the doors of deeper perception be opened, the texts urged. But John struggled desperately to still his thoughts during meditation as required. Flickering visions continued to haunt him...

The Amulet engulfed in shimmering violet flame, its angry heat searing his palms as he tried futilely to contain it. Ghostly apparitions fleeing and screaming soundlessly as buildings crumbled around him, strange winged shadows swooping through the smoke...

Each time the traumatic memories threatened to engulf him, John doggedly redirected his focus to memorizing the intricate glyphs in the texts and the precise alignment of the ritual tools. He was no longer the naive youth who had failed so catastrophically all those years ago. The painful lessons of that tragedy had honed him, body and spirit. He clung to that hard-won wisdom like a life raft as he delved deeper into the shadowed unknown.

When exhaustion threatened to overtake John, Talia gently guided him away from the faded pages to eat and rest. Though she voiced no open criticism, John sensed her unspoken worry over the unhealthy obsession that gripped him. But she still prepared the bitter potions he needed without complaint, massaging herb-infused oils into his temples to ease the throbbing headaches induced by endless study.

Her unwavering support was John's sole comfort amidst the all-consuming darkness. He had known the quest would change him, force him to embrace power and knowledge long forbidden. But he had not anticipated how close the lure of it would bring him to the precipice of mania...

Desperate for greater insight, John also met with renowned scholars and sages who had devoted their lives to unraveling the Amulet's arcane secrets. Most refused to help once they learned his intent, insisting any attempt to wield its primordial magic was doomed folly at best, opening the gates to catastrophe at worst.

But a few dissenting voices echoed John's own intuitions...and fears. The ancient sorceress Sybilla invited him to her remote forest sanctuary for counsel.

"There are always two paths," she intoned as they conferred around a moonlit brazier. "The Amulet's destructive potential is vast, yes..." She traced a gnarled finger down strange symbols etched on the ancient codex before her. "But hidden within its wildfire heart is the seed of life itself. Few indeed have the wisdom and clarity of mind to cultivate it without being burned."

The sage Ekarius also confirmed John's dangerous course could lead to either salvation or damnation when they met again in his cluttered study. But he urged John to seek beyond dogma and cultivate a beginner's mind. "The mystery the Amulet holds is not one of force," Ekarius mused, "but surrender..."

John clung desperately to these fragmentary insights during his darkest moments of doubt. Perhaps the key was not sheer power or unwavering will as he had believed. But wisdom — knowing precisely when to unleash the magic and when to restrain it. His past failure had sprung from reckless ignorance, grasping blindly for control. Now, at last, he was ready to understand.

But understanding alone would not be enough, John feared as the fated hour drew inexorably nearer. He focused his meditation fully on opening himself to the hand of Providence — surrendering to a wisdom far greater than his own. Only by attuning himself to the guiding force of Destiny could John hope to wield the Amulet without unleashing calamity once more. If he relied on his limited self alone, darkness or madness lay ahead...

The winding path was revealed to him slowly through dreams and visions. He walked through flames, but the fire illuminated rather than destroyed. Thunder shook the heavens but left clouds ripe with rain that nourished the soil. The Amulet blazed brightly in his hands, but its searing heat transmuted into crystallized light...

When the moon swelled at last to completion overhead, all preparations were complete. The ritual tools shone, aligned precisely as the ancient texts dictated, vessels brimming with the gut-wrenching elixirs needed to open the doors of perception.

In the darkness before dawn, John

came to Talia to make his farewells, uncertain if he would return. Wordlessly, she pulled him into a fierce embrace, then placed a woven bracelet around his wrist — an anchor binding their spirits no matter what lay ahead. John clasped her hands one last time, praying this would not be the end. Then he turned and strode alone into the waiting gloom.

The ritual site called to John from deep within the shadowed forest. In that liminal place between worlds, he would, at last, take up the power that had broken him long ago and let its searing flame forge him anew. Gripped with terror and exaltation, John walked onward into his destiny, ready to face the dragon without...and within.

CHAPTER 10

John entered the mage briefing room, the familiar smells of coffee and parchment bringing him back to his early days as an agent. How far he had come since then, through failure and redemption. Now, he studied the large map of London intently, marking locations where Victor might be hiding.

Recent intelligence suggested Victor needed access to ley line convergence points to unlock the Amulet of Corsair's full destructive power. John circled three possibilities — an old cemetery, the catacombs beneath Parliament, and the British Museum. Powerful arcane energies flowed beneath each one.

In John's mind, he pictured Victor

seated in a shadowed library, obsessively studying ancient texts, seeking the ritual's missing key. John knew they had to stop him before he solved the riddle. He tried to place himself in Victor's shoes, analyzing memories of their past duels. Victor favored deception and misdirection over direct magical attacks. But John was no longer so easily fooled...

"Why is Victor so obsessed with the Amulet?" asked Mage Carter, an eager young recruit. "Wouldn't any powerful dark artifact serve his plans?"

John nodded, gazing thoughtfully at the map. "It's not just power he seeks. Victor resents authority in all forms — he believes dominating others proves his worth. The Amulet symbolizes limitless power unrestrained by rules or morality. Victor craves that level of control."

John himself had stared into that abyss once before. The memory still haunted him, a mixture of shame and hard lessons learned. But no more. He had turned from that path for good. Now, to ensure Victor found no refuge in the darkness.

Over the next several hours, John delved into the history of Victor's early life, seeking clues to his motivations. As a youth, Victor showed great magical promise — top marks, popular with peers, and respected by teachers. But over time, unhealthy obsessions took root. Most notably, an unrequited love for a brilliant classmate turned to bitter resentment toward society.

Victor found validation from a charismatic Dark Wizard who encouraged his ambitions and thirst for secret knowledge. They performed dangerous magical experiments delving into subjects banned at the school. Each forbidden spell and success fueled Victor's arrogance and contempt for rules.

John saw parallels to his own mistakes — thirst for glory, impatience with restrictions, and desire to prove himself leading to terrible misjudgments. But where Victor had fully descended into wickedness, John still had a chance at redemption. This was his opportunity to face the sinister shadow he almost became and ensure the light prevailed.

The hour had come. John straightened his mage robes and entered the briefing room. The team gathered there turned, conversation dimming. John saw a mix of solidarity and wariness in their faces. Some still doubted if he was ready for this.

John began presenting his attack plan but faltered as haunting memories surfaced unbidden. Crippling self-doubt threatened to resurface. Then, deep resolve rose within John like a phoenix from ash. He launched into an impassioned speech from the heart:

"I know many of you still harbor doubts," John said. "You question if I'm truly ready to confront the man who defeated me once before. To lead you all into peril against an enemy who haunts my past. You have every right to doubt me. I failed in my duties as a mage once. My mistakes enabled a great evil to be unleashed."

John paused, gathering himself before continuing. "But since that tragedy, I have sacrificed everything to prepare for this moment. I have studied case files late into the night and honed my skills far beyond what they were. I have looked deep within myself, faced harsh truths, and reforged my will. I carry the shame of my past mistakes always. But rather than break me, that shame drives me to earn back your trust and respect. To prove I have learned from my failures. I would not be standing here today if I hadn't sacrificed everything to be ready for this mission."

John met each mage's gaze in turn. "So I ask you — give me this chance. Put your faith in me once more, and I swear I will fulfill my duty. I will do whatever it takes to make things right and end this threat for good."

The mages glanced between each other, inspired by John's raw honesty and dedication. This was not the same prideful man who had failed them before. The Head Mage scrutinized John a moment longer before nodding.

"You've earned the right to show us what you're made of, John," he said gruffly. "I can see you are not the man you once were. Seize this opportunity that has been afforded you — and know we are behind you."

John swelled with gratitude. These people had once counted him among their best. Now, they were giving him the chance to prove himself again. He would move heaven and earth to justify their faith. This time, he would not fail.

After finalizing the mission plans, John stopped by the apartment that had once been his and Marissa's home. Stepping inside, nostalgia washed over him as memories flooded back — shared meals, laughter, dreams discussed late into the night. It seemed another lifetime now.

John heard shuffling from the bedroom. Marissa must still be here, packing up the last of her things. John hesitated, unsure if he was ready to face the bittersweet confrontation. But before he could slip away, Marissa appeared in the living room.

"John," she said with surprise that quickly turned to wariness.

"Marissa," he replied awkwardly.

"I was just...picking up a few things."

They stood in silence a moment before attempting stilted small talk — about the weather, Marissa's work at St. Mungo's. Finally, Marissa sighed.

"It feels strange being here again together," she said. "This used to be our haven. Now it's just a place that used to be."

John nodded heavily. "I've missed it. Missed...us."

Marissa wrapped her arms around herself. "It changed after you got obsessed with hunting Victor. You grew cold and closed off. I lost trust."

John looked down. "You were right to doubt me. I became consumed by it all. I shut you out when I should have drawn you closer. I'm truly sorry, Marissa. For all the pain I caused."

Marissa met his eyes. "We both made mistakes. But perhaps it's not too late to heal."

John's throat tightened with emotion. "If I somehow make it through this, I promise I'll make things right between us. No more secrets or grudges. Just openness and honesty."

Marissa gave a sad smile. "I can see shades of the good man I once loved." She touched his arm gently. "I wish you luck, John. Truly."

They shared a bittersweet hug before going their separate ways again. John strode out reinvigorated. Defeating Victor had always been about saving society. But now, it was also deeply personal — reclaiming all that had been lost. This was his chance to become whole again.

Heavy mist swirled as John arrived at the hidden rendezvous point. He and Talia had traded coded messages setting the meeting spot — they took no chances with operational security. Through the haze emerged the lean silhouette of the spirited young Spellsmith.

Talia's face broke into a fierce grin at the sight of John. "Ready to go hunting?"

Despite himself, John laughed. "Your enthusiasm is as intoxicating as ever."

Together, they checked weapons and equipment — caster gauntlets, protective charms, and Disillusionment gear. John's smile faded as he ran through pre-mission checks on autopilot, his thoughts clearly elsewhere.

Talia paused, watching him closely. "Something on your mind?"

John hesitated before confessing

his visit with Marissa. Talia listened thoughtfully as he described the emotional conversation.

"I'd nearly given up hope of reconciling with her," John admitted. "But now..."

"Now you have a spark of hope," Talia finished. "Hold onto it. Let it guide you through the battles ahead." She squeezed his shoulder. "You're nearly there."

John nodded, tamping down the flare of optimism. He couldn't lose focus. "And yet, doubts remain," he said quietly.

Talia's expression turned fierce. "John Constantine Gray, you listen to me. You have been to hell and back a dozen times over. You have conquered enemies and trials that would have destroyed lesser men. You have faced your deepest shame and emerged stronger." She gripped his hands tightly. "If anyone is ready for this final confrontation, it is you."

John clung to her words like a lifeline,

drawing courage from her steadfast faith. Talia had stood stalwartly by his side through endless adversity. Without her light guiding him, he would never have made it this far.

"We will win this," she declared. "Victor's night is ending. Have faith."

John's spirit rose, buoyed by her wisdom. Together, they would defeat the darkness. They traded quips and hyped each other up for the fight ahead, spirits high. Ready for anything, they donned disguises and slipped off into the night. The final battle awaited.

Fog still clung to the docks as John and Talia approached the abandoned warehouse, its slumped form barely visible against the water's dark ripples. This was the place John had faced utter defeat years ago, the Amulet ripped from his hands. Most men would have been haunted returning here. But John felt only cold purpose as he strode toward the decrepit building. The past could not chain him anymore — he was not that broken man. Tonight, it ended.

Water lapped against weathered pylons as they slipped inside. John's senses strained in the musty darkness. Cargo crates loomed like misshapen giants through the gloom. This had been Victor's lair once. Faint magical traces hung in the air — signs of recent activity. They were in the right place.

John signaled Talia to cover the left flank while he moved right. Wands drawn, they crept between the crates, hyperalert for any ripple in the silence.

Too late, John detected the trap — a shimmering magical barrier that exploded with painful force as they crossed its threshold. Like granite bands, the hex clenched his muscles in paralysis. Beside him, Talia writhed against the curse's grip, her cry strangling in her throat. Through the haze of pain, John sensed rather than saw figures emerging from the shadows, wands aimed directly at their hearts.

The sight should have filled him with despair as failure loomed again. Instead, John's mage instincts took over, honed sharp as a blade by endless training for this very moment. With intense focus, he analyzed the paralyzing hex, identifying weaknesses in the arcane weave. As their attackers closed in, John mentally isolated the countercurse.

"Arcteuro Contramino!" he bellowed through clenched teeth. The bands of energy holding him shattered. John rolled clear a split second before a curse scorched the ground where he lay. The shadowy figures fell back in surprise.

Pressing the advantage, John launched a volley of stunners while Talia slipped into the darkness. In moments, their ambushers lay scattered and unconscious across the concrete. Talia let out a victorious shout, clapping John on the back with a grin.

"Amazing work! You totally turned it around on them."

John shook out his tingling limbs, exhilarated by their narrow escape. The John of old would have panicked, allowing despair to paralyze him further. Now, he had reacted with perfect focus and discipline, even amidst chaos. His mage instincts had returned, at last, sharper than ever. This small triumph fortified his spirit for the greater battles ahead.

Leaving their vanquished foes bound by steel cords, John and Talia pressed deeper into the warehouse. As they descended a metal staircase, the air grew heavier, crackling with ominous arcane energy. The fine hairs on John's neck prickled. Victor was near.

Reaching the final stairs, he stilled his mind with long, measured breaths. Training, preparation, and experience would guide him now. Fear had no power over him anymore. With Talia shadowing his steps, John descended into the vault passage, each footfall echoing off cold stone.

He and Talia marched onward boldly, souls united. Darkness still lay ahead, but its power was fading. This was what he had sacrificed all for — a chance to seize destiny with both hands. That chance had come at last. And this time, John would seize it.

CHAPTER II

The stairs opened into a vast chamber lit by the sullen crimson glow of a towering obelisk. Strange glyphs and half-glimpsed shapes moved across its surface. John hurtled through the battered door, sprinting up the crumbling steps two at a time with Talia on his heels. The decaying tower trembled around them as Victor's chaos spread. They had to reach the top before the Dark Wizard completed his cataclysmic ritual.

With a final burst, John exploded onto the tower's peak. The howling wind threatened to hurl him back into empty space as he took in the scene. Victor stood atop the ceremonial dais, arms raised triumphantly as infernal light streamed from the Amulet cupped in his hands. His mad eyes found

John's across the platform.

Victor turned slowly, pale eyes glinting with malignant humor. "Welcome to your demise, John." His voice echoed eerily around the domed room. "Did you truly think you could challenge me and live?"

John stepped forward, wand leveled unwaveringly. "Your tricks no longer work on me, Victor."

Victor smiled coldly. "We shall see." He began circling them like a patient predator. "I must compliment you on making it this far. Few have proven so... irritatingly resilient."

His voice remained low and mocking, carefully selected words crafted to unnerve and deceive. Once, such calculated psychological attacks would have needled John, stoking self-doubt and insecurity. Now, the verbal barbs washed over him, hollow and transparent ploys. John had finally seen through the mask to the desperation beneath.

"You're out of maneuvers," John replied calmly. "It's over. Last chance — surrender the Amulet."

Victor's smile twisted into a hateful sneer. With a scream of rage, he lashed out, unleashing a storm of dark fire. John deflected it with a shimmering shield charm and advanced inexorably. Bolts of light burst from his wand, spell chains and curses John had painstakingly crafted for this very duel. Beside him, Talia transformed into a snarling panther, slashing at their foe with razor-sharp claws.

Victor easily dodged Talia's claws. "You're too late!" he shrieked. "The power is mine!"

In answer, John slashed his wand through the air, severing Victor's connection to the Artifact. The light winked out, and it tumbled from his grasp.

"No!" Victor dove for the Amulet, but John summoned it to his own hand. For a heartbeat, he feared its volatile power would overwhelm him again. But he had conquered his doubts and regrets. The Amulet's fury could not crush his spirit now.

Snarling in rage, Victor unleashed a barrage of deadly curses. John deflected them, the Amulet's magic amplifying his own. Bolts of energy lit up the ruined tower as they dueled furiously across the dais. Though Victor attacked with reckless fury, John retained focus. He would not be goaded into making mistakes.

Step by step, John pressed back the Dark Wizard, using his agility and creativity to gain the upper hand. He transformed debris into animals that harassed Victor from all sides. When Victor vaporized them, John harnessed the dispersing energy into binding chains. His innovative spells kept Victor off balance.

But Victor fought on with the tenacity of madness, too lost in vengeance to accept defeat. The duel seemed deadlocked until a blasting charm crumbled the edge of the dais where Victor stood. As he teetered precariously over the abyss, John disarmed him with a wordless Expelliarmus.

Weaponless, Victor could only scream curses as John immobilized him in conjured shackles. It was over at last. John stood above his defeated foe, chest heaving with exertion. He had finally fulfilled his vow to stop this threat.

But as he retrieved Victor's wand, the Dark Wizard began an incantation. Too late, John realized he was tapping directly into the Amulet's power source. A rumble shook the earth as Victor poured every last shred of magic into one final act of spite.

Through the cracked floor, John glimpsed the sea recoiling from the shore far below. Victor was summoning a catastrophic tidal wave to wipe this land from existence.

Mind racing, John attuned himself to the forces Victor had unleashed. As the massive wall of water surged inland, he redirected its power skyward with a guttural cry. The uncontrolled deluge exploded into the air harmlessly.

The effort left John drained. As the last foaming drops rained down, his knees buckled. Somewhere, he heard Victor's triumphant cackle cut short. John's eyelids fluttered closed. He had ended the threat but at great cost. Darkness took him.

Sensation returned slowly to John's stunned body. He felt hands clutching at him urgently and heard Talia's voice as if from a great distance. With agonizing effort, he forced his eyes open.

Fiery destruction raged around them. He lay collapsed beside the radiant Amulet, its power raging unchecked now that its master was dead. The energy surged and ebbed erratically, lashing out to engulf buildings in purifying flames. Only the shelter of Talia's enchantments had saved them, but it could not last.

Despair threatened to crush John

beneath its weight. He had sacrificed everything, only to fail again when success was within grasp. How could he hope to contain power so wild, so endless?

Talia gripped John's face between her hands, eyes blazing. "Listen to me!" she shouted over the chaos. "You can do this, John. I know you can!"

John wanted to believe her, but he had nothing left. The gnawing doubts returned. The Amulet had broken him once before. He lacked the wisdom and strength to tame it.

As if reading his thoughts, Talia shook him. "You are not the man you were! Remember what you have learned!" When John turned away in shame, she grabbed his wrist, placing his palm directly onto the Amulet's shimmering surface.

Every muscle in John's body seized at the contact. It was like grasping lightning — primal energy lanced through his veins, searing and irresistible. The power concentrated the essence of life itself.

Memories and emotions surged through John's mind in a psychedelic torrent. He teetered on the precipice of oblivion.

Through it all, he heard Talia's voice anchoring him. "You can control this!" she insisted. "I have faith in you!"

With her words kindling a spark of hope inside him, John focused his fractured consciousness wholly on the Amulet. There beneath the wild destruction, almost drowned out by the fury, he sensed it — a resonant harmony aligned to life's essence. The song of creation itself.

In his mind's eye, John saw flashes of his past failures and regrets parading before him. He had run from them for so long, crushed under the shame. Now, he embraced those experiences, forgiving himself at last. In love, there could be no fear.

The Amulet flared brighter, and this time, John did not turn away. He surrendered himself utterly to its fiery heart. For one eternal moment, he was lost in the vortex...

until finally, it released him, transformed.

John opened his eyes with a gasp. The furious power was quieted. By surrendering his guilt and shame completely, John had extinguished the Amulet's destructive fire, leaving only purifying light. Already, he could feel healing energy radiating outward, restoring the broken city. He rose unsteadily, reborn.

All around John, his allies stirred as the Amulet's light knit together flesh and stone. Cries of amazement echoed as its wisdom sank into every living mind. They gazed at John with awe, sensing the transformation he had undergone. He had conquered demons within and without.

As the people gathered around him, John knew words were inadequate for the mysteries revealed to him. But as his eyes found Talia's, shining with pride, inspiration came to him.

"True power lies not in force," John told the assembled crowd, "But understanding.

Controlling the Amulet required surrender, not strength. I share its lessons now with all who would listen."

John extended his hand, and the Amulet rose gently. He sensed now its destiny was not raw power but teaching. In the right hands, its wisdom could transform the world. John vowed to walk that path, Talia steadfast at his side. The war was ended. A new era of healing had begun.

CHAPTER 12

Soft dawn light filtered into the vaulted chamber as John placed the Supranium Amulet on its pedestal one final time. Intricate glyphs of power, wisdom and protection carved into the ancient stone walls flickered as the first beams of sun illuminated them. This sacred place had been chosen long ago to guard what could not be allowed loose in the world.

The Amulet pulsed with dormant power, its fiery heart now tamed. John had vanquished its destructive potential by surrendering his own guilt and shame. Now, it would pose no more danger.

With great care, John enacted the sealing rituals. He traced each glyph with a feather's tip, softly murmuring the sonorous words of power. Motes of dust swirled in the shafts of sunlight as resonant notes echoed off the chamber walls. The very air seemed to vibrate with purpose as John wove the enchantments to encase the Amulet in an impenetrable sanctum.

None must ever abuse its power again. The lessons it taught were not brute force but wisdom through compassion. John worked slowly, honoring each word and gesture until, with a final resonating toll that rang through mind and soul, the Amulet was secured out of reach. The long burden John had carried was lifted.

Soft footsteps sounded behind him. He turned to see Marissa entering the chamber, eyes bright with emotion. By her side was the daughter he hadn't seen in five long years. After so many years estranged, she had insisted on witnessing the Amulet's sealing. The bonds between them now could never be broken, having overcome such darkness together.

Marissa embraced John tenderly. John picked up his child and swung her around. Her peals of laughter healed his ravaged soul. As they held each other, words of love poured forth. They spoke of the pain that drove them apart, the paths they each had walked since, and through it all, the undying care that had endured in their hearts. Light and shadow, joy and sorrow — all essential threads woven into the tapestry binding their lives as one.

"I'm so proud of you," Marissa later whispered, head resting on John's shoulder. "You've conquered the demons that haunted you, becoming the extraordinary man I always knew you could be."

John stroked her hair softly. "We've healed what was broken and found wholeness together."

Marissa touched his cheek gently. "A new beginning awaits us." Side by side, they turned and walked into the light.

The mage headquarters buzzed with

frenetic activity when John arrived, but sudden silence fell as all eyes fixed on him with unconcealed awe. He had departed their ranks under a cloud of scandal. Now, he returned redeemed beyond question.

As John walked down the aisle, lenses flashed, painting him in scattered moments of brilliant light. Nearby, mages reached out to clasp his shoulder, murmuring earnest gratitude and congratulations. The air thrummed with energy awaiting release.

Miles emerged from the crowd, head bowed in shame. "John, I must apologize," he began haltingly. "The cruelty and jealousy I showed you over the years..." His voice broke. "There are no excuses." He met John's gaze with watery eyes and extended a hand. "Can you forgive me?"

John clasped his old friend's arm without hesitation. "Of course. Our true friendship can and will be rebuilt."

Miles clutched John's hand tightly, overcome by emotion. "Thank you, John. I vow to become the man you see in me."

Fanfare sounded as the Head Mage approached, bearing an ornate medal, ruby gemstone glinting in the torchlight. The crowds' excited whispers crescendoed to thunderous applause as he halted before John.

"John Constantine Gray, you have fulfilled your duties with the highest honor, redeeming this institution's reputation through your valiant deeds." He lowered the medal around John's neck. "We formally reinstate you as Mage First-Class with deepest pride and gratitude."

As cheers rang to the rafters, John raised a hand. "The real triumph was finding wholeness within. I accept this honor as a symbol of hope's eternal light guiding us ever higher."

Stowing his medal safely, John departed to make one final solemn farewell. The graveyard's serene silence calmed his churning emotions as he approached

Claire's modest plot. Kneeling, John placed a bouquet of violets by the weathered headstone. Fingers trailing the carved name, he allowed the long-held grief to flow forth until tears mingled with the soft rain misting his cheeks.

"Your faith gave me strength when I had none," John murmured. "You always believed I could confront the darkness and win redemption. I will carry that trust always."

At long last, the shadows lifted fully from his heart. Claire's guidance had led him from the valley of despair back into the light. Soft blossoms nodded as if whispering, "Until we meet again." With soul at peace, John walked onward.

The Head Mage could not conceal his disappointment when John declined his offer of a prestigious promotion. There were still chapters left in John's life, but his mage tales had reached a fitting conclusion.

In the archives, John penned a

reflective farewell in his mage record:

"I have faced the demons within and without, ever striving these long years to fulfill my duties to my utmost ability. Now, I shall pass the torch to the next generation, who will lead with their own formidable strengths. My trials have set me free, replacing regret with hard-won wisdom. The time has come to soar to new heights unfettered by the past."

After signing his name, John tucked away the book to be preserved for posterity. Though departing active duty, his experiences would guide those who came after. His legacy was secure.

Talia waited by the threshold when John emerged, bag in hand. Though ready for new horizons, parting ways weighed heavily.

"This is not goodbye, but a new beginning," John told her, voice ragged with emotion. He gripped her shoulders as if to convey through touch what words could not. "I can never repay what I owe you. You inspired me when all seemed lost."

Talia's eyes glistened as she hugged John fiercely, rubbing his back in slow circles as though comforting them both. "We will meet again. Our spirits are intertwined for all time by the trials we overcame."

They held each other for a long moment, words unnecessary. Then John slung his bag over his shoulder and walked toward the rising sun, not looking back. The time had come to face the possibilities of the future unburdened by the past.

Warm sunlight on his face lifted John's spirit as he stepped outside, inhaling his first breath as a free man. He left behind the robes and trappings of duty that had cloaked his identity for so long. What lay ahead now was a boundless horizon of potential.

Before journeying onwards, John had one final farewell to make. He cut a solemn figure weaving through the cemetery's familiar headstones until he reached two bearing the names forever carved into his heart.

"Mother. Father," John greeted softly, laying a hand on each cool memorial. "I've made peace with the troubled past that long haunted me. The bitterness is swept away, leaving only cherished memories behind. You shaped the man I became, and for that, I thank you."

With those healing words, John turned and strode into the dawning light. His trials had set him free at last. The shadows of regret could touch him no longer. He was the master of his destiny now.

As John walked onward, the verdant landscape seemed imbued with new beauty and meaning. He paused to appreciate each delicate wildflower and birdsong with fresh gratitude. The shadows he had endured made the light more precious.

John crested a hill overlooking his childhood home. With fond nostalgia, he recalled climbing the old oak's branches and playing Mages and Dark Wizards around the yard with imaginary friends. Each memory was a faded snapshot capturing a moment that together told the story of his beginnings.

When John arrived home, his tawny owl greeted him joyfully, bearing a small parcel. Inside, he found Claire's worn leather journal brimming with affirmations praising his kindness, wisdom and strength of character in her gently looping script.

John wept tears of joy reading the moving passages, any last doubting voices banished forever. Though he had lost his way at times, the truth dwelled within him all along. Now he was home and could embrace that fully as he began life anew.

With limitless possibility shimmering on the horizon, John packed his essentials and set out on the open road, eager for whatever adventure lay ahead. Each step was an act of faith, propelling him forward into the great unknown. But he walked on boldly, spirit renewed and unbound. The hero's journey came full circle as he strode into the future unshackled by the past.

The setting sun gilded the road ahead as John trekked on tirelessly. He was the master of his destiny now. The trials he had overcome forever changed the trajectory of his life's course. Though challenges awaited, John embraced each coming day with open arms. The future was a story still to be written. And this time, the ending would be on his terms alone. With blazing eyes, John marched forth, knowing his long trials had set him free at last.

Olivia Huntington has always been fascinated by magic, myth and adventure. As a child, she spent countless hours dreaming up stories of heroes overcoming monsters and finding hidden treasures. This sense of wonder followed Olivia into adulthood, compelling her to obtain degrees in ancient history and occult lore. After working for years as a magical artifacts historian, she decided to try bringing some of the incredible tales from her research to life in fiction.

When not crafting her next thrilling fantasy saga, you can find Olivia camping under the stars, exploring ancient ruins, or searching dusty libraries for magical secrets lost to time. She loves immersing herself in nature and absorbing legends from cultures across the globe to fuel her imaginative stories.

Olivia currently resides in a rambling old house in the countryside that provides daily inspiration. She shares the creaky halls and mysterious locked rooms with three adorable cats and one very patient husband. The only magic she can reliably perform is turning endless cups of tea into completed book chapters.